To Lucas, Alicia seemed to be the center of everything.

He thrust the rogue notion away. The Chandler Organization was the axis that held his world together. Alicia was business.

Just business.

Don't touch her, his callous side said. *Don't get closer than you have to in order to make this work.*

But he couldn't help himself. He bent down, cupped the back of her neck. "What can I do to make you more at home?"

heart lurched when he saw all the questions r beautiful golden eyes. *What am I doing How do I handle being your wife?* But he 't allow things to implode now. Not when d already come so far.

He just had to win her over again, right? That's all there was to it.

Dear Reader,

Have you ever met a guy with deep dimples and a killer smile? Did you ever hope that this demigod could maybe, *just maybe,* fall for a normal girl, just like most of us, in some parallel universe?

That's how Alicia Sanchez feels. She's not a princess or even queen of the prom. Yet, when Lucas Chandler, billionaire playboy, walks into her life, it's love at first sight, even if she's thinking that there's absolutely no way a man like him will ever give her the time of day. Luckily, Lucas isn't any old heartthrob….

So join Everyday Average Alicia and all the other women who've fallen for that perfect guy and hoped that, perhaps, one day, by some miracle, he might feel the same way, too.

Here's to your own happy endings!

Crystal Green

www.crystal-green.com

THE PLAYBOY
TAKES A WIFE

CRYSTAL GREEN

Silhouette

SPECIAL EDITION®

Published by Silhouette Books

America's Publisher of Contemporary Romance

SILHOUETTE BOOKS

ISBN-13: 978-0-373-24838-4
ISBN-10:   0-373-24838-5

THE PLAYBOY TAKES A WIFE

Copyright © 2007 by Chris Marie Green

All rights reserved. Except for use in any review, the reproduction
or utilization of this work in whole or in part in any form by any
electronic, mechanical or other means, now known or hereafter
invented, including xerography, photocopying and recording, or in
any information storage or retrieval system, is forbidden without
the written permission of the editorial office, Silhouette Books,
233 Broadway, New York, NY 10279 U.S.A.

This is a work of fiction. Names, characters, places and incidents are
either the product of the author's imagination or are used fictitiously, and
any resemblance to actual persons, living or dead, business establishments,
events or locales is entirely coincidental.

This edition published by arrangement with Harlequin Books S.A.

® and TM are trademarks of Harlequin Books S.A., used under license.
Trademarks indicated with ® are registered in the United States Patent
and Trademark Office, the Canadian Trade Marks Office and in other
countries.

Visit Silhouette Books at www.eHarlequin.com

Printed in U.S.A.

CRYSTAL GREEN

lives near Las Vegas, Nevada, where she writes for Silhouette Special Edition and Harlequin Blaze. She loves to read, overanalyze movies, do yoga and write about her travels and obsessions on her Web site www.crystal-green.com. There you can read about her trips on Route 66 as well as visits to Japan and Italy.

She'd love to hear from her readers by e-mail through the Contact Crystal feature on her Web page!

To Mary Leo and Cheryl Howe:
the best two pals a workaholic could ever have.

Chapter One

The minute Lucas Chandler stepped out of his limousine and onto the hard-packed earth of Rosarito, Mexico, he was swarmed.

Flashbulbs assaulted him, and so did the questions—most of them encouraged by an introduction to this press gathering from David, his half brother and the CEO of The Chandler Organization, otherwise known as TCO.

"How much money did you donate altogether to get Refugio Salvo running, Mr. Chandler?"

Flash.

"Why the sudden interest in an orphanage, Mr. Chandler?"

Flash.

"Can you comment on what happened in Rome with Cecilia DuPont and the police, Mr. Chandler?"

Yeah, there it was—the kind of query into Lucas's party-hearty lifestyle David had been attempting to circumvent.

Lucas forced a smile for the next photo, already sick of today's charade. What he wanted to do was get inside the orphanage and leave the cameras in the dust. And, no doubt about it, there was plenty of *that* covering the dilapidated buildings around them.

But one glance at stone-faced David told him that this was only the beginning of Lucas's new life: the turning over of a fresh public-relations leaf.

Why the hell had he agreed to this again?

Oh, yeah. To be a decent person. And then there was also the small matter of saving TCO.

Slipping into his most comfortable disguise—the charming act—Lucas shot his brother a brief glance, then dived in to answer questions. David, for his part, stood back, hands folded behind him, as cool and smooth as the Italian designer suit he was wearing.

Lucas ignored the confinement of his own suave wardrobe, all but boiling under the many layers of material. It was warm for December down here.

"Ladies and gentlemen…" Strategically he flashed his dimples, making the lone female reporter light up with a blush. "Thanks for being here. And, when I tell you that I won't be divulging dollar amounts, I'm sure you'll understand. Suffice it to say, that we gave a lot to the Angeles Foundation here in Mexico to buy the land, construct the orphanage and supply them with everything they'd need to keep the children in safe comfort. You can be assured that Refugio Salvo will be well taken care of in the future, too. There're also plans for more sites farther south, but that's still on the drawing board."

One of the male journalists raised his hand. "Rumor is that you'll be cliff diving in Acapulco after you visit the orphanage. You gonna take some orphans with you, or what?"

Ah, the Funny Guy. There was one in every crowd and one in every backside.

As Lucas reined in his temper, most of the other reporters lowered their cameras and notebooks, laughing. Even David, whom Lucas believed was made mostly of granite, smiled. But the gesture was more rueful than amused.

The female journalist answered for him. "That's great, Denham. Why don't you give Mr. Chandler a little credit, huh? He's got enough sense to keep the kids away from all that 'daredevil playboy' stuff." She glanced at Lucas hopefully.

Did they think he was some out-of-control idiot? Obviously. Maybe it was good that he'd promised David that he would lay off all his notorious thrill-seeking for a while.

Still, even the female reporter—Jo, that was her name—didn't look as though she truly believed he could behave himself.

"Thank you, Jo," he said, knowing he could use her as an ally. She was from one of TCO's media outlets, a newspaper that consistently tried to balance out the tabloids and the other entertainment sources that covered Lucas's colorful adventures.

At the reporter's modest shrug, Lucas turned to the others. "This is a time to find some serious answers for the troubles these orphaned boys are having. *That's* why I'm here—to check up on the progress and make plans for even more."

It wasn't the entire truth. He was also trying to show off the "new and improved" Lucas Chandler. TCO required it and so did—

Lucas tensed. *Don't think about the old man,* he told himself. *You're doing this for business and business only.*

Riding a crest of deep-seated frustration, he added, "I'm here to provide aid for these kids who might otherwise end up on the street without any education or vocational skills."

Censured, the reporters subjected Lucas to more pictures, and he tolerated it like the man his family had always expected him to be. The man he really wasn't.

Flash. Pop. Each burst of illumination needled into him.

Finally, a pleased David made his way over, putting a hand near his mouth so the reporters couldn't see what he was privately saying to his brother.

"Good start. Just so you know, they're running late in the orphanage because of a greeting the children have put together for you. They'll be ready in about twenty minutes."

Lucas presented the journalists with his back. "In twenty minutes, I'll need five shots of tequila."

Out of the corner of his eye, he saw some nuns wearing wimples and stark long skirts with white blouses. They disappeared behind a stucco wall of the orphanage.

Disappear, Lucas thought. What he'd give to be able to take a breather behind that wall, too.

David cleared his throat to regain Lucas's attention. When he had it, he fixed his ice-blue eyes on him. Funny how a twenty-eight-year-old genius could put a man who was three years older in his place with just a condescending reminder.

"Don't tell me," Lucas said, "that I should be used to this kind of attention. I can handle the paparazzi, but this is different. This is business."

"Yes, I know it's not your thing, but we agreed."

"Yeah, yeah." Agreement, sha-mee-ment.

"Mr. Chandler?" called an impatient reporter.

Something snapped in Lucas. No more questions, dammit. No more apologies for his recently abandoned lifestyle or justifications for "the playboy's trip to the orphanage."

"You take over," he muttered to David while walking away.

"Luke—"

"Buddy, you're the brains of this outfit, so dazzle the crowd with 'em." Lucas winked, just to convince David—and himself—that he had his position as the "face" of TCO under control, that he was still the pretty boy who fetched publicity while David actually ran the place.

But it was about *good* publicity this time, Lucas thought.

Too much of his PR had been negative. Especially

lately, with all those nonfamily-friendly wild-romance-in-the-streets-of-Rome scenarios he'd been enjoying with Cecilia DuPont, this month's starlet. Impulsive scenarios that shed a red light on TCO.

As he left the media circus and headed toward the spot where the nuns had disappeared, he heard David assuming control of the press. Good man. He knew how much of this crap Lucas could handle before blowing.

Shortly after arriving at the wall, he ducked behind it, finding a cast-iron gate. In back of that, there was a flagstone path strewn with vivid pink flowers. A fountain burbled in the near distance. Sure sounded peaceful to him.

Opening the gate, he slid behind it before he could be spotted by anyone, then walked over the path toward the running water.

The fountain was in a side courtyard where red bricks and iron benches hinted at a mellowness Lucas had been craving. Like a collapsing wall, he crumbled onto one of those benches, loosening his tie and rolling his head around to work the cricks out of his neck.

Now this was more like it. No damned cameras, no pressure. Just for a second—

A soft giggle hit the fragrant air.

He cocked an eyebrow and glanced around at the thick foliage surrounding the courtyard.

"Peekaboos," said a child's voice from one of the bushes.

An orphan? Lucas couldn't help grinning. Hell, as long as the kid didn't have a lens aimed at him, he could deal.

A devilish titter followed. It reminded Lucas of how

he used to laugh when he was younger. Everything had been a joke to be told, a riddle to be solved, a game to be played. He still sort of subscribed to that theory, even if it got him into trouble more often than not.

Suddenly a woman's voice came from behind the bushes. "Gabriel? *Dónde está?*"

The foliage rattled as Lucas spotted a few strands of black hair spiking out from the leaves.

Two nuns scuttled into the courtyard. They chattered in Spanish, seemingly panicked.

"Gabriel!"

They stopped as they saw Lucas rising to a stand, hands in his pants pockets. He merely grinned and shrugged, hating to give the kid's position away.

One exasperated nun addressed him in English. "A guest? You are to come in the front door, sir! Not the back."

Thrilled that she hadn't recognized him, Lucas eased her a grin. "Sorry."

The nun raised a finger to say more, then stopped, reconsidered and sent him her own sheepish smile. "It is okay, sir."

It worked every time, Lucas thought. The Dimples.

Meanwhile, the other nun—a woman with chubby cheeks and a lively gaze—had caught sight of the little boy's hair. She parted the bushes, only to jump back when a golden-skinned child with wide brown eyes exploded out of the leaves, squealing. His hair splayed away from his head, wild and free, just as playfully ornery as Lucas suspected the rest of him was.

Much to the nuns' horror, Gabriel climbed into the

fountain and proceeded to splash around, sending waves of water at them while they tried to approach. The boy's defense worked wonderfully, because it seemed that the nuns thought they would melt if they got water on their clothing.

Finally he took pity on the ladies. They were, after all, of good quality, even if they didn't appreciate the fine art of child's play.

Approaching Gabriel from the back, Lucas scooped him up, putting a stop to all the shenanigans. Water dripped from the child's clothes, but Lucas didn't mind. His suit would dry.

"Hey, little guy," he said, "time to stop being a squirrel."

The child looked up at him, and Lucas blinked back. In those dark eyes he saw the same troublemaking, misunderstood expression that stared back at him from the mirror each morning, the glint of rebellion in a confused gaze.

Another female voice rang through the air. "Gabriel?"

"*Now* she comes," the first nun said, checking her skirt for water damage.

The chubby-cheeked nun merely caught her breath and flapped a hand in front of her face.

Gabriel squirmed, but Lucas wasn't dumb. He kept a hold of him, spinning him around to stand on one of the benches.

The boy held up his hands and laughed. "*Mucho gusto!*" He had mile-long eyelashes, chubby, round, smudged cheeks and a secondhand shirt splashed with water and old dirt.

A tweak of sympathy—that's what it was—forced Lucas to reach out and ruffle the kid's hair. Cute bugger.

"Gabriel," said the more exasperated nun, "please speak your English. And you are soaking and dirty. How will you be ready for the show?"

The boy stubbornly shook his head, turning to Lucas. "No show," he said, repeating the nun's word.

English. Suddenly Lucas remembered David's preparatory briefing: part of the orphanage's educational program included ESOL—English for Speakers of Other Languages.

A sound investment of the company's money, David had said, because it would allow bilingual children more opportunity and make TCO heroic.

Lucas liked the sound of that. It was a solid deal, even if a boy as young as Gabriel might not have learned that much since Refugio Salvo had only been running for about nine months.

His thoughts were interrupted by the arrival of that third woman. She was out of breath, her head bare, black hair curled in disarray down to her shoulders. Her light brown skin was flushed, her dark gold eyes wide.

She dressed like a nun but…no wimple. Maybe she was one of those novices or whatever they called them.

As they locked gazes, she held a hand to her chest, as if surprised by something.

Lucas's blood zinged and swerved through his veins. Instinctively, he took things up a notch and offered what the papers called "the smile to end all smiles," the ultimate way to charm any woman who caught his fancy.

Even a wannabe nun? he wondered. Say it ain't so.

Her stark clothing couldn't conceal the lush curves of her body. Around her wrist a charm-laden bracelet gleamed. Maybe this order wasn't traditional, choosing to forgo dressing in regular habits and accessories.

At any rate, Lucas thought, she's off-limits. *David, Dad and the board of directors would go ballistic if you outdid yourself and big-bad-wolfed a future nun, of all people.*

In welcome, she broke into her own smile, blushing while she allowed her hand to fall to her side as she gathered her composure. The color of her cheeks brought even more animation to her delicate, innocent features: a gently tipped nose, full pink lips and dark angel-wing lashes.

"I see you've met Gabe," she said breathlessly. Her English was very good, with barely the trace of an accent.

The cranky nun interjected. "Lord, help the man now."

"Sister Maria-Rosa…" said the chubby-cheeked one. Then she turned to the newcomer. "We were all playing 'Splash the Authority Figure,' and Gabriel was the winner."

The woman nodded. "It seems you put up a good contest, Sister Elisabeth."

"I always do." The nun looked like some kind of cherub as she rolled her eyes in resignation.

The new woman walked toward Gabriel. The boy was fairly hopping with excitement at her presence.

"You having fun with your friend?" she asked, frowning slightly at the boy's drenched clothing.

Gabriel reached out for a hug. The woman freely gave it to him, not seeming to mind that she would be dampened, too. When she pulled away, Lucas tried to keep his eyes off a wet blouse that was now hinting at the lines of a simple slip underneath.

Future nun, nun, nun, he told himself.

After she helped Gabriel down from the bench, it took her only a few seconds to realize that she was less than fully covered and she awkwardly crossed her arms over her chest. Good thing, too, because Lucas had been dreading having to embarrass her by pointing it out. It'd been tough enough to keep his gaze averted.

"Gabriel," the nun named Sister Maria-Rosa said, "we need to change your clothing now." She sighed. "What are we going to do with you?"

The novice stepped forward, arms still protecting her front. "I can—"

"No, Alicia—" Sister Elisabeth said, gently taking Gabriel by the hand and leading him away "—You already have many responsibilities. Don't worry about Gabriel."

They hadn't addressed her as "Sister," but maybe that was typical for a wannabe.

The nuns nodded at this woman named Alicia—a four-syllable name as opposed to three, Lucas noted—as they left. The little boy turned around and waved back at them.

"*Adiós,* Miss Alicia. Bye-bye, man."

Lucas waved, too, along with four-syllable Alicia.

"He's really a good boy." She looked at him, blushing an even deeper red, then glanced away. "Most of the time."

Lucas didn't know what to say, because if Gabriel was anything like *him*, as he suspected, she was dead wrong.

"But you were handling him very well," she said, raising a brow and grinning.

Damn.

He laughed, just to set himself back to balance again, to send away the thrust of a taboo attraction. "But I don't have to control him twenty-four hours a day."

Her face fell, and he realized that maybe she'd been sizing him up for a possible adoption.

Right. *Him.* That was a funny one.

He shrugged off his coat and offered it to her. With a grateful nod, Alicia took it.

"You don't mind?" she asked. "I don't have an extra change of clothes here and—"

"I don't mind a bit." Well, yeah, actually, the hound in him *did* mind, but Lucas wasn't about to admit to any carnal thoughts around someone bound for the church.

"Thank you." She put it on, bringing an end to the best thing that had happened to Lucas all day.

She tilted her head, gauging him again. Then, as if he'd passed some kind of test, she stuck her hand out.

"I'm Alicia Sanchez and I'll be your group's guide and hostess. We're so pleased to have you at Refugio Salvo, sir."

As he took her hand in his for a greeting, his skin tingled, sizzled.

Attracted to an angel, he thought. It was definitely something new, even for him.

* * *

As the stranger's hand enclosed hers, Alicia's heart kicked at her chest. It'd been doing that since the first instant she'd seen him, and she still hadn't recovered.

Unable to get enough of looking at him, she noted every detail: Fancy tie, shirt, shoes. Well groomed. His jacket smelled good, too, like spicy soap, clean and heady.

He was a lot taller, so much that she was forced to lift her chin to meet his gaze. The color of his eyes startled her—a deep violet, just like the flowers that had grown in the small garden of her *abuelita*'s house back in San Diego. His light brown hair was a little long and ruffled, carefree in the breeze. His body...

Alicia tried not to look, but she couldn't help noticing that he was strong, wide-shouldered and muscled like an athlete.

His grip tightened, and she realized that she'd been staring, her skin goose-bumped and flushed from the inside out.

Quickly, she let go of him, gaze trained on the ground. She shoved the hand that had been holding his, into a jacket pocket, wishing it would stop blazing with heat.

Then, donning a civil expression, she distanced herself from the visitor. Right away she saw the glimmer in his eyes fade a little, as if he were second-guessing something. Then he also took a step backward.

"You're with the billionaire?" she asked, making conversation. Easy enough, with his affable personality.

It was obvious that he was here with Lucas Chandler.

She knew the reporters were out in front now, taking pictures and asking questions before they all came inside Refugio Salvo. But why wasn't he with the rest of the crowd?

He gave her an odd glance, then sent her a high-wattage smile in answer. She just about pooled into herself right then and there. What was happening? Dizziness, flushed skin, a giddiness she couldn't explain...

"I'm looking forward to meeting him," she said, ignoring the blasts of heightened awareness shooting through her.

"Because he's so handsome?" He was teasing.

"Well, that's what the female cooks here say, among other things."

Cocking an eyebrow, he sat on a bench, looking pretty entertained with her comment. "They say that, do they?"

"It's not all that important. I'm not one for TV or tabloid nonsense, anyway. But still..." She blushed, laughing at her all-too-human curiosity. "I am wondering about him."

Especially because he had money. Wait—that sounded wrong. It wasn't that *she* wanted any of it. If Mr. Chandler were in another charitable mood, the orphanage itself would be much better off after another donation.

He was smiling at her again. Dimples. My, my.

They were such nice, deep dimples. Semitrucks could park in them.

Yet...was this man sort of flirting with her? Alicia

wasn't sure, but she should put a stop to it. *Now.* No, really, *now.* She wasn't a nun, but she might as well have been with all the promises she'd made to herself. No sex before marriage—never again. As a volunteer who worked side by side with the women of Our Lady of the Lost Souls at the orphanage, she did her best to be a good role model for the children.

And then there was also a very personal need to remain chaste….

"So the nuns volunteer at the orphanage, too?" he added, interrupting her musings.

Press time. She put on her best PR voice. "Yes, the order teaches academics and sees to the boys' spiritual needs. Regular workers—" like her "—run the facility and oversee the ranch work since each boy, whether he's just old enough to start chores or mature enough to work with the horses, has scheduled responsibilities and training."

"You're all a very caring group of people."

Why did he suddenly seem so…sad? Or did he look guilty? Alicia couldn't be sure.

The splashing of the fountain became the only sound. She rushed to cover the tension, wanting everything to run smoothly.

"It's our pleasure," Alicia said. "We're really happy to love and be around these children."

Months ago, she had volunteered to work here, renting a small house off the profits from the impetuous sale of her deceased grandparents' home. She had pleaded with the orphanage's director to be the one who played hostess to the billionaire, to be the one who secured a bundle of money for their needs.

She had to succeed in her goal for the orphanage today, to do whatever she could to be a decent person and fight for their requirements. *Had* to. The more money she raised, the more she could forget about the stain on her soul left by her *abuelo*'s dying words.

"So you've met him?" she said to the visitor, testing the waters. "Lucas Chandler? Do you think he's a kind-hearted sort of guy?"

The man seemed taken aback, but then he fought a smile, clearly knowing something Alicia didn't. "Kind-hearted? I suppose that depends on when you catch him."

"Oh." Heaviness settled on her shoulders.

"What?"

He leaned forward, encouraging her. From just his smallest movement, Alicia's pulse kicked, sending a swirl of scrambled yearning to her chest. But passion wasn't on her daily schedule. Not when it was so important for her to wait for a respectable marriage; it was the only way to experience what came between a man and woman. Marriage made sex pure and right.

She drew the jacket closer around her body. "Truthfully? We were hoping that he's one to part easily with his money."

Well, that had come out wrong. Maybe she was just too flustered around this man; Lord knew she was more articulate than this. She'd meant to say that she hoped he would be generous to the children, that's all.

And she could tell that she'd surprised him with her

words—her greedy-sounding, awful words. Well done, *muchacha,* well done.

His shoulders had stiffened. She rushed to correct herself but was interrupted.

"Alicia!"

She turned around to find Guillermo Ramos, head of the orphanage, rushing toward her. His crown of salt-and-pepper hair fluttered with the speed of his gait and his slender mustache twitched. Someone was in a snit.

"It's not quite time to start the greeting," she said in English, not wanting to leave their visitor out of the loop. "The children should be ready in a few more minutes."

"No, we are clearly starting now." Guillermo stopped suddenly, hand to heart. "Mr. Chandler, I am Guillermo Ramos. We have talked on the phone."

Alicia glanced at the stranger, who had gotten to his feet, hand outstretched toward Guillermo.

Mr. Chandler?

Good heavens, she was crushing on the billionaire?

"Good to see you, Señor Ramos," he said.

Gulp.

Alicia anxiously fiddled with the charm bracelet she always wore, but Guillermo was all smiles.

"I see Senorita Sanchez has been entertaining you during our delay—which I apologize for profusely," he said.

"Our future Sister Alicia's been doing an exceptional job." The stranger—no, *Lucas Chandler,* the billionaire—turned to her. Now, with the title and money, he seemed…different. More imposing and definitely even more off-limits. "We were just small talking."

Yes, she thought. Due to her ill-chosen words at the end of their conversation, she had obviously gotten smaller and smaller in his estimation.

And…future Sister Alicia? Who did he think *she* was?

"I am glad to hear it," Guillermo said. "But you must know that Senorita Sanchez is not with Our Lady of the Lost Souls." Here he laughed a little. "She is not even a Catholic, but we are fortunate that she is working in our company."

At those words Lucas Chandler's eyes lit up, changing him from an average visitor to everything the other orphanage employees had been whispering about.

Playboy. Ultimate bachelor. Devil in disguise.

"Excellent." He leveled that lethal dimple-edged smile at Alicia once again. "That's some excellent information to know."

She swallowed hard, feeling as if he'd whipped the jacket right off her.

Exposing everything she'd been covering up.

Chapter Two

As the Chandler party returned from the horse stables on their grand tour of Refugio Salvo, Lucas kept his photo-op smile in place. The cameras caught it with their freeze-frames, trapping him in the flashes yet again.

Alicia was at the head of the group, leading them toward the main building, which had been sparsely decorated for the upcoming holidays. There they'd be having an informal meet and greet with the children, who had already welcomed Lucas into their home with a sweet rendition of "What a Friend We Have in Jesus" before Alicia had guided them onward. They'd seen the state-of-the-art school building with its computer room, the mini gymnasium with basketball hoops and hardwood floors, the library stocked with the most recent and popular titles, the cozy quad-occupancy rooms in the cottages.

Money. It could work wonders.

Lucas stuck his fists in his pockets. Idly, he watched the way Alicia moved, her hands clasped behind her back, her hips swaying under the oversized jacket and full, dark skirt as she traveled the dirt path that led from the paddock to the main house. The mild air, scented with hay and sunlight, toyed with her black curls. When one strand of wild hair tickled her cheek, Lucas imagined smoothing it away, tucking it behind an ear and receiving one of her gorgeous smiles in return.

But she hadn't been smiling so much during the tour. Not after she'd told him the real reason she was interested in Lucas Chandler.

We were hoping that he's one to part easily with his money.

Join the club, honey, he thought.

He'd tried to forget how his chest had clenched when she'd said that. But why was he surprised? People liked him for what he could supply, whether it was cash, amusement or a good headline to laugh over in a tabloid.

That was all anyone had ever expected of him, so what was the big deal?

Hell, maybe he just wanted more from a woman who'd at first seemed a little different from the rest.

They arrived at the casa's back door, where one of the older boys—a teen with slashing eyebrows, crooked teeth and long scraggly hair—greeted them.

Camera flashes bathed the teen and Lucas as they shook hands.

Then, as everyone started entering the building, Alicia thanked them, inviting the crowd to eat and mingle.

The journalists wasted no time in attacking the spread: burritos, small tostadas, punch and cookies placed carefully on plates over the paper tablecloths. The boys stood nervously around the poinsettia-strewn room, plastic cups in hand, waiting to play host to their patron.

While going inside, David gave a laconic nod to Lucas. His brother was obviously happy about how today had gone. A flare of satisfaction caught Lucas in its spotlight and he glanced at the ground, hiding his reaction.

After the teen had entered, too, that left Lucas, who had stepped back outside to hold open the door for Alicia, the last of their group.

She hadn't moved from her hostess spot. In fact, Lucas got the feeling that she'd been watching him the whole time. He could tell by the intelligent depth of her gaze, the tilt of her head that maybe she'd gleaned something about him that he wanted to hide. Something that most people never caught on to.

He shut the screen door, arming himself with the Dimples to throw her off the scent of what she might've seen: Lucas's need to get this right, his fear of always being a joke.

"A job well done, Ms. Sanchez," he said lightly.

Narrowing her eyes a little, she held his jaunty stare. "I've been waiting to apologize to you. For the entire tour, I kept wondering what you must think of me."

"Don't sweat it. You thought I was a regular guy, I thought you were going to be a nun...."

"I'm talking about my comments. Please don't let my failure to say what I really meant reflect on the orphanage. We really are grateful for everything you've done. I hope you don't believe we aren't appreciative."

Caught by her honesty—Lucas wasn't really used to it from anyone except David—he leaned against the casa's stucco, the texture scratchy against the fine weave of his shirt.

Before he could answer, a preteen bounded out of one of the cottages, his all-white clothing spotted by colors.

"*Ay*, Roberto," Alicia said, stopping him. She laughed, glowing, as she straightened the boy's wardrobe. "Did we interrupt your painting?"

Roberto nodded, shooting a glance to Lucas, who shrugged in confederacy with the boy. Being late was cool with him.

"You." Alicia sent Roberto off with a soft, good-natured push. "Just don't let Sister Maria-Rosa see you."

After Roberto tore off, Lucas watched Alicia. She was still smiling in the wake of the boy's presence.

How could he ever doubt this woman's intentions? She seemed so openhearted, so guileless.

But...damn. It wasn't as if Lucas had great insight into character. There was a lot of anecdotal evidence that could prove his lack of judgment.

"Well..." Alicia said, whisking her hands down over her skirt, removing the imaginary wrinkles. "I suppose we should be getting inside."

Disappointment dive-bombed him. "Yeah—" he adjusted his tie "—I suppose we should."

Neither of them moved.

Instead, they waited as the wind hushed around them, the sun sinking closer to the horizon.

Both of them laughed at the same time, a quiet, intimate admission that neither of them felt like going anywhere.

"I've had it with reporters," Lucas said.

"I can tell."

"Not that I don't want to greet more of the kids. Don't get me wrong."

"Of course."

His eyes met hers and, for a moment, everything around them stopped—the wind, the rattle of branches.

For the first time in his life, Lucas didn't know what to say to a woman. But he didn't really want to be talking, anyway. In this pocket of stolen time, he was content just to look at her, to see the gold in her eyes shift with thought and sunlight. How had she come to be here, wearing these frumpy clothes and hanging out with nuns?

As if reading his mind, she looked away and touched her bracelet, almost as if it gave her something to concentrate on.

"So what's your story?" he asked softly. "What made you decide to volunteer for this kind of social work?"

Another strand of hair grazed her cheek, her lips. Lucas couldn't take his eyes off her mouth, the lush promise of it.

"I've found," she finally said, "that I'm good at working with young people."

"I can see you enjoy them."

The startling hue of his eyes seemed to press into her, digging for more information. She fidgeted, her skin too aware, too flushed with thoughts she shouldn't be having.

The forbidden nature of them kicked her brain into high gear; all the impulsive reasons she'd moved from the only home she'd known in the States to come down to the resort area where her parents had met.

"When my grandparents passed away, I realized what I needed to do with my life," she said, voice thick with emotion. She missed them so much, wanted them back so badly. "They raised me in San Diego, but, after they died, staying there didn't appeal to me." She swallowed, tacking on a harmless falsehood just to cover the reminder of why she was really in Mexico. "Not when I realized there was so much to be done down here."

"Your grandparents raised you?"

Alicia flinched, crossed her arms over her chest. "My mom and dad…passed out of my life. A long time ago."

Another adjustment to the truth.

Lucas Chandler stood away from the wall, so devastatingly handsome, so confusing to her. Couldn't her body just ignore those dimples, that inviting gaze?

He ambled closer, a growing hunger in his eyes, his interest in her so obvious that it almost took her breath away.

Closer…mere inches away.

Inhaling his scent, she got dizzy. Her head filled with scenarios, hints of fantasies—

Skittish, she took a casual yet significant step away.

She didn't want to offend him by assuming he was hitting on her, but she was trying to be a careful girl. Especially lately, after her view of life had been so blasted apart by what her grandfather had told her as he lay dying.

From a few feet away, she heard Lucas chuckle. When she chanced a look at him, she saw a vein in his neck pulsing.

Stop him from getting close again. "I think it's time to go inside now. The children are waiting and—"

"We shouldn't be standing out here by ourselves." His grin wasn't amused so much as wry. "I know. One photo with me and there goes your reputation. You're obviously held in some esteem around here, and we don't want to ruin that."

"That's not what I meant."

But he was right. The last thing she needed was this man standing only a few tension-fraught feet away from her, his skin giving off heat and the smell of musk and soap. She'd been around enough to know his type; he could make a girl think that whatever trouble they could get into was right.

Back when she was sixteen, she'd learned this well. Swayed by an older crowd—one her grandparents didn't know about—she'd given in to peer pressure on a summer night with a boy named Felipe.

And she'd liked it. So much. Too much.

Afterward, she'd been dogged by all the moral lessons she'd learned from church and her grandparents;

she'd even wondered what was wrong with her that she'd enjoyed it so much.

Needing some kind of stabilizer, Alicia had made a vow to wait for intimacy again until marriage. Then she could be a good wife, and sex would be respectable with her husband.

She was no angel—not even close. But now, more than ever, she tried her best to be.

There was a cryptic flicker in Lucas's eyes. It seemed to make him change his mind about being so close to her, because he grinned tightly and nodded while he turned away. Like the gentleman she'd seen all day, he held open the door for her to enter the building, his gaze suddenly a million light-years distant.

The sound of happy chatter greeted her, and she was drawn to it—charity, a cleansing of the soul.

But as she passed by Lucas Chandler, she met his gaze, seeing that it was anything but removed. Seeing that it was so filled with a lingering admiration for her that she couldn't help picking up her pace and fleeing.

An hour later, most of the boys had retired to their rooms, signaling the end of the reception. The reporters had been ushered away by David long ago, when the food had become less than a novelty and they'd gotten itchy to take pictures again.

Thank God for their absence, because Lucas was done with business for today. Come to think of it, he'd actually lucked out by avoiding the press in his more private moments. He'd all but lost his head out there with Alicia, almost forgetting what a picture alone with him would've cost her.

He really *hadn't* been thinking clearly, not with the way his body had been reacting to hers, growing more responsive with every step he'd taken toward her. And he was used to getting what he wanted from women too easily not to be miffed by her reluctance.

Still, he'd respected her refusal to turn their alone time into something more, had seen the warmth in her eyes when she'd talked about being with the kids. Lord knew Lucas didn't hang out with many people who had ambitions beyond planning the next party or acquiring the next "big thing" that would make them a Donald Trump overnight. She was refreshing, so why change her into one of his social casualties?

Especially since he was supposed to be turning over that new leaf.

As David summoned the limo and took a phone call outside, the last of the orphans said goodbye to Lucas. Gabriel, the kid who'd been so friendly at the beginning of the day, had seemed oddly shy at the reception, adhering to Alicia—who'd kept her distance from across the room—the entire time.

But, now that the excitement had died down, the dervish Gabriel was back, zipping over to Lucas with the verve of a tightly packed hurricane. He was carrying the jacket Alicia had been wearing.

"Hi," he said, giving the material to Lucas and shuffling from foot to foot.

Alicia followed him over, and Lucas perked up even more.

"He's practicing English on you," she said, acting as if he hadn't invaded her personal bubble earlier.

Maybe her polite cheer would force Lucas to be a good boy around her.

"Well, then…" He hunkered down to eye level with Gabriel. "Hi, back to you, too."

That was the boy's cue. Gabriel started to rattle off a breathless description of all the food he'd eaten today, and Lucas listened attentively. Somewhere in back of him, an enterprising reporter clicked away with a camera. Obviously, at least one of them hadn't gone home, after all.

Photo op. Lucas had stumbled into a nice one, hadn't he?

It wasn't until Gabriel stopped chatting and started watching him with those big dark eyes that Lucas realized his throat was stinging with an emotion he couldn't identify.

What the hell?

Brushing it off, he chalked it up to seeing evidence of the good those English lessons had done.

He abruptly stood, averting his face, ignoring thoughts of all the numb days that had been linking his existence together.

His sight settled on his brother, who was lounging by the doorway, tucking his phone into a suit pocket, face pensive.

Keep it together, he told himself.

By the time Gabriel tugged on Lucas's pants, Lucas had collected himself enough to turn around again.

The child stood there, dark eyes wide and playful. "Come on, come on. Hide-and-seeks."

As the child jumped up and down and tried to lure Lucas out of the casa, a nun from across the room called to the boy.

"It's time for chores, Gabriel. Say goodbye now."

The child frowned, looking as if he didn't comprehend why the fun had to end. Then, without warning, he turned to Alicia and fired a barrage of upset Spanish words that Lucas couldn't translate. His tone was choked, his hands fisted in front of him as he punched the air.

Lucas's chest tightened with concern, with empathy.

But when Alicia patiently reached out to smooth Gabriel's spiky hair, just the way you would your own child, the boy paused, at first shaking his head and denying her. But as she spoke soothing words, Gabriel allowed her to get closer, closer.

Carefully, she drew him to her, continuing to murmur as she hugged him and smoothed a hand up and down his back.

Thank God, within a few seconds, Gabriel had stopped, his head resting on her shoulder, one hand fisting the material of her blouse.

In his eyes Lucas saw those reflections again, the painted shadows of his own heart buried beneath this kid's chest. The need to find someone who could help him, too.

The words slipped out before Lucas could rein them in. "We'll hide-and-seek next time, Gabe, huh?"

He didn't know why he'd said it. Dammit, when would he ever be coming back here?

But then that beautiful smile lit over Alicia's lips, and Lucas knew it wouldn't take much more persuasion.

"See you soon, then, Mr. Chandler," Alicia said, leading Gabriel away and acting calm enough to fool him into thinking that nothing dramatic had just happened with the kid. "Thank you for everything."

Lucas nodded, unable to stop himself from appreciating the way her curvy hips swiveled under that shapeless skirt. She gave real nice form to it, that was for sure.

Before reaching the door, she sent him one last glance, and the power of it just about bowled him over. All she did was smile a little, and his world tipped.

What was it about her? In that smile it seemed as if she could read his mind, slip beneath his skin, whisper inside his head.

I know you're hurting, he imagined the smile saying. *And I understand.*

After they'd left, Lucas finally took a breath.

Realizing that he'd been holding the same one for what seemed like hours.

David had already gone outside by the time Lucas had said his farewells to the orphanage director. The Brain was waiting for his brother near the limo, where they had a view of the property: the main building, the annexes and the cottages, the chapel, the stables.

Arms crossed casually over his chest, David assessed Lucas, eyes a cool blue. With his stoic/casual pose, he looked like a stone-carved cowboy.

"Guess who called?" David said.

Lucas knew the answer before being told. "What's the damage from the old man this time? Or is he announcing another future stepmom who's two years older than I am?"

Well practiced in this line of conversation—one that never went anywhere—David kept his silence. Instead, his body language said it all: the loose limbs that spoke of a man in control of his own destiny, the slight tensing of his jaw that hinted at tension between the brothers. David was a big fan of Lucas's hands-off business approach; he didn't mind running everything while Lucas flashed his smile to the world at large. It was Lucas's majority holding in the corporation's stocks—a contract-tight promise his father had made to his first wife that included always seeing that Lucas, the firstborn, would own the company—that got to the Brain.

"Just spill it," Lucas said, tired of waiting.

"He wanted an update. Wanted to know if today's events were enough to impress Tadmere and Company."

Tadmere, the family-oriented American media empire they were trying to acquire. Owning them would revitalize TCO, as well as give them more of an avenue to compete with the print rags and news shows that made a living off stalking Lucas. But the current, very pious owners were balking at turning over "their baby" to a company supposedly led by a man of Lucas's reputation. It was Tadmere—and that scandalous Rome trip—that had prompted this whole personal PR campaign to make him look like a "nice guy."

"And what did you tell him?" he asked nonchalantly, as was his habit. His dad hated when he did that.

And Lucas thrived on it.

"I told him things went perfectly." David glanced at his Rolex and stood away from the limo. "He was happy about that, Luke. Really happy."

A splinter of euphoria stabbed at his chest, making him bleed a little. It happened every time the old man seemed to be coming around, ever since he'd survived the stroke. But, even now, Lucas wasn't about to get too giddy; Ford Chandler would return to prehealth-scare form soon enough. Lucas wasn't about to set himself up for a fall.

"I'm sure you can imagine the happy fireworks going off in me," Lucas said.

David sighed and shook his head. "Come on. You and I both know that, this time, maybe Dad will come around to appreciating you. I, for one, am sick to death of the way things are. And don't deny—" David held up a finger to silence Lucas just as he was about to protest "—that you are, too. Suck it up this time and don't get all rebellious against the guy. He's sticking out an olive branch, these days. Would you just take it?"

"And what would sucking it up entail, David?"

"Just doing more of what you did here today. That's all. Did it hurt so much?"

In the back of his mind, he heard Gabriel speaking English to him, saw all the boys lined up by the food tables and smiling in an effort to impress him.

Him—the notorious Lucas the Lover.

Respect, he thought. How would it feel to finally have it?

But it was impossible to come clean with David at this point. After all, it'd been tough enough to admit to his brother that he'd gone overboard in Rome with Cecilia DuPont and that he needed to cut the shenanigans.

And it'd been awful to admit it to himself, too. Admit that, more than anything, he craved one kind damn word from a father who didn't give out many of them.

In response to that, Lucas had made a career out of being apathetic about the business his dad had raised from the ground up with his heart and soul. TCO was the son Ford Chandler favored best, so why didn't he expect resentment from Lucas?

Resentment. God, it wore him out. He was weary from fighting a father who'd seemed to age fifteen years in the last month. The last time Lucas had seen his dad—hell, it was the day the competing tabloids had come out with that picture of Cecilia dancing in all her naked glory in a fountain, with a champagne-swilling Lucas cheering her on—the man had looked almost done. *Finito*, as Lucas's Italian buddies would've said.

His fed-up father had been in a hospital bed in the penthouse of one of his New York buildings, skin pale from the pains Lucas had brought on. That was the day Lucas had realized that he might not have much time to show his dad he could be an actual success—not the punchline of the family.

"I think we accomplished a lot here," Lucas said. "I wouldn't say no to doing more of it."

There. Underplay it. Don't let them know how much it would mean for you to be taken seriously.

A small grin lifted the corners of David's mouth, and Lucas knew he'd said the right thing.

"Today was just the first step," his brother said. "It'll take more than a few charitable photo ops to erase that bad-boy image you've got going."

The memory of his father's exhausted sighs and the slump of his shoulders—disappointment—edged into Lucas. He could do more, all right.

Still, he didn't want to seem too excited. He couldn't go that far yet. "You have something in mind, Einstein?"

"I've had some ideas today." David's eyes went a bit dreamy, the pose of many genius brainstorms that had kept TCO afloat. "It'd be perfect if you could do something to put the world's—and Tadmere's—doubts to bed for good. What we need to do is make you a pillar of society."

"We've had a good start."

"It goes way beyond the orphanage. I'm talking about a life change. A total tabula rasa so no one remembers Rome or Paris or the many screwed-up headlines you've inspired."

Lucas bristled, mostly because the words were coming from his younger sibling. Mostly because they were true.

"Mammoth task," he muttered.

"Not really."

David was watching something in the distance, so Lucas turned around.

Without warning, his heart pinged around his chest and jumped up to lodge in his throat. Alicia Sanchez was walking hand in hand with a work-clothing-garbed Gabriel to the stables, swinging arms and laughing together.

"You got along with her real well," David said. "And you're good with kids, especially that one."

Slowly Lucas turned back around, shoulders stiff and wary, his blood racing.

David held up both hands. "Trust me on this—if you could even do one thing like convince the public that you're capable of a stable relationship with a decent woman, Tadmere would be ours. It might take some time for them to see what a wonderful monogamous man you've become, but… What can I say? Love changes even the wildest of miscreants. Then maybe, in the future…kids."

"You've got to be kidding." But even as he said it, a part of Lucas—the one that'd felt numb today, the one who'd cried out for a father's respect—didn't completely shut out the idea.

"Think of how the world would look at you," David added. "A reformed rake. People love that."

Monogamy. *Respect.* A relationship. *Respect.*

Respect, respect, respect.

That was the bottom line, the one prize that had eluded Lucas for so long that it seemed like a dream.

"She's beautiful." David again, damn him. "If you could be paired with a 'nice' woman like her…pure gold."

"Yeah, and, if the public found out that this was just a relationship built on the need for good PR, I definitely would come off looking even worse than before."

"Lucas—" David cocked a stoic eyebrow "—think of those Rome pictures with Cecilia. How could you possibly come off as more of a rake? Besides, we've got our publicity machines to cover for us."

Embarrassed anew to have been caught nearly in flagrante delicto by the press, Lucas glanced over his shoulder. Alicia and Gabriel were disappearing behind the buildings.

But that wasn't the only reason he couldn't help looking.

Fantasy merged with reality just for one pulse-stopping moment: Alicia's smooth cheek against his palm, her curly hair between his fingers, her lips against his…

But then the rebuttals rushed in, pounding against his skull. Good girl. Playboy. *Right.*

"Forget it," Lucas said, his tone brooking no argument.

"Listen, celebrities do this kind of thing all the time for good ink when they want to polish themselves up. Can you imagine the great press, even from the sources we don't own?"

And it'd be just a business decision, Lucas added. *Nothing different from any of the other safe relationships—dead ends—that you've had with every woman up until this point.*

As Gabriel scuttled into the open, laughing and trying to break free, Alicia emerged to catch him, hugging him to her. Lucas's stomach somersaulted.

Why? Because… Well, hell, because he was having

doubts that he even had the ability to be a one-woman guy. All the press's snide opinions testified to that.

Right? That's the *only* reason he was feeling so weird.

"It wouldn't hurt to talk to her to test the waters and see how she might react to such an idea, anyway," David's voice said.

The words drifted over Lucas as he kept watching Alicia, the woman who intrigued him and, Gabriel, the child who he suspected was so much like him.

Something like a family, Lucas thought as an unfamiliar emotion filled up the emptiness behind his ribs. What if…

Lucas turned to his brother, ending the discussion with a lethal glare.

Yet that didn't mean he wasn't hearing David's logic over and over in his own mind as they drove back to his five-star resort room, where he ended up pacing the floor most of the night.

Chapter Three

When Guillermo Ramos had contacted Alicia last night, requesting that she entertain Lucas Chandler at the orphanage for one more day, her belly had scrambled with excitement.

She told herself it was more because she was *that* much closer to securing additional money for the orphanage than anything else—like, say, seeing the billionaire again.

Ridiculous, she thought now as they rode horses over the sun-dappled property. He was so far out of her league it wasn't even funny. Plus, she had more important things than flirting to think about.

She snuck a look at him, hoping he wouldn't notice. The same wind-ruffled hair. The same piercing eyes.

He seemed at home, sitting expertly in the saddle in his faded jeans, the reins threaded through his hand. Even though Mr. Chandler had told her that he wanted another gander around the place in order to see how additional donations could be utilized, Alicia found herself tongue-tied right now, unable to "sell" her own ideas about what Refugio Salvo could use.

But she would get over it…just as soon as she could overcome this strange shyness enveloping her. Was it because there were no cameras and the lack of them made everything much quieter, more real? Less like she was putting on a show?

"Look west, Mr. Chandler." She pointed in that direction as they halted their horses. It was an expanse of grassy land, much like what they were on now, but it was cut off by a barbed-wire fence with a sign that said No Trespassing in Spanish.

"Neighbor's property?" he said, easily controlling his roan gelding, Ackbar, who was dancing around.

"Yes, and possibly more land for the foundation to purchase for the ranch."

With one last glance at the land, he paused, then prodded Ackbar into motion again. She caught up to him, and they rode side by side. He seemed deep in thought, so she didn't bother him unnecessarily. She didn't feel the urgency to.

And that was interesting. Even though she hadn't spent more than a few hours with him, there was a certain comfort level in place. It was almost as if she'd known him before and they'd slipped right back into a companionable flow upon his return. Alicia had never experienced anything like it. She was naturally good with people, sure, and that's why Guillermo was using her as a hostess. Yet there was always that invisible shield with strangers—a force you didn't see but a barrier that was definitely there, all the same.

But not with Lucas Chandler. No, there was a different, unspoken something hanging over them…a humid atmosphere she'd been trying to avoid thinking about.

The sounds of chirping birds and moaning saddle leather accompanied them as he took the lead. He seemed confident in where he wanted to go, so Alicia went with it, ready to correct their course if need be.

"Ms. Sanchez," he said, his voice blending with the smooth, grass-laced air, "may I ask you a question? And, if you don't want to answer, that's fine."

She straightened in her saddle, friendly but on alert. "Ask away."

"I'm just wondering, Ms. Sanchez…or Alicia. May I call you that? Alicia?"

"Of course."

He smiled to himself. "I love how everyone says it down here. A-lee-see-a. It's like a song."

She laughed. "Was that your big question?"

"No. I'm just thinking about yesterday, especially when I asked you about how you came to be a volunteer here. The orphanage doesn't pay you? Sorry if that's too personal—"

"Don't worry. It's a part of how Refugio Salvo works, and you'd want to know." Pancho, her mount, nickered, and Alicia absently patted the horse's neck.

"The orphanage can afford salaries for most of the staff—administrators, cooks, groundskeepers. But the sisters consider their work here to be part of their calling, freely given. Just like I do."

"You should be compensated."

She flushed, thinking how a paycheck would definitely help in day-to-day living but would also take away some of the significance of what she was doing. Charity. With a salary, her intentions of giving without taking just didn't seem to count as much.

"Not to seem ungrateful, Mr. Chandler, but—"

"The money's coming whether you take it or not."

Alicia didn't glance at the man next to her, but she didn't have to. She felt his gaze on her. Her skin heated, flaring to confusion.

What was driving him to stick around to see the details of what the ranch needed? Some of the orphanage staff whispered it had to do with all the cameras that had followed him yesterday, but Alicia didn't want to believe that.

Maybe he was trying to make up for something he felt badly about, just as she was. Maybe he was attempting to find purpose, too. But there was one thing she could guarantee: his trip to Refugio Salvo hadn't been designed to allow him to hide from the reality of a life left behind. That was her own cross to bear.

Her father…her mother…her shameful past.

Many times she'd even wondered if the piety she'd been raised with was forcing her to punish herself for how she'd been born. For her parents' carnal crimes that her *abuelo* had told her about. There were so many times she thought that the circumstances of her birth made her less of a person....

Mr. Chandler had grown quiet in his own right as he gauged the land with narrowed eyes. He wore an expression that gave her pause—so serious, his brows drawn together, his lips tight.

"Is something wrong?" she asked.

"I'm just now realizing how much can still be done." A beat passed, then a mirthless grin settled on his mouth. "Now that the camera flashes have worn off, it's a clearer view."

"You've been a true supporter," she repeated. But somehow she doubted it was getting through to him.

"I haven't contributed half as much as you, and that's humbling, Alicia."

For a naked second, she thought she saw a chink in his armor. She'd detected it yesterday, too, but he'd closed it up so fast that it'd almost been subliminal.

"As long as we all do our part," she said, "the children will flourish, Mr. Chandler."

"Lucas. Just call me Lucas."

They resumed their ride, neither of them speaking. He was back to that thinker's pose, and she wondered what exactly was causing all the seriousness. He seemed to catch on to this, because before she could take her next breath, he sent a sudden, devilish grin to her, encouraging his mount to a trot.

What had that sudden change of mood been about?

Not to be outdone, Alicia urged Pancho ahead, laughing, then hunching over her horse's neck and signaling him to a gallop.

Almost immediately he did the same, until they were neck and neck, flying over the grass.

A bubble of amusement expanded in Alicia's chest, then popped. She urged Pancho on and soon she realized that Lucas was veering toward a massive oak tree, its bare branches spread like a canopy, a haven from the mild sun.

When they got closer, she saw that there was a picnic table covered with a red-and-white-checked cloth. Silver bowls and a vase of wildflowers dominated the china.

Flabbergasted, she dismounted, cooling Pancho down. Lucas followed her example, and she couldn't help glancing at the spread with contained anticipation.

Laughing at her obvious impatience, he came and took Pancho's reins, allowing her to sprint to the table to finally get a closer look.

When the horses had been taken care of, Lucas sauntered over, having given them freedom in the grass.

"A picnic?" she said, her heart just now returning to a semblance of normal thud, thud, thuds.

Then again, with every step he took closer, her pulse started picking up again.

"It's snack time." He went over to a silver bowl on top of a smaller table and washed his hands, drying them off with a fluffy towel. "Come and get cleaned up. I thought you might enjoy something flown in from Bella Sofia. It's an Italian restaurant I like in San Diego. You enjoy Italian?"

"Who doesn't?" Still stunned, she moved over to her

own silver bowl, the rim delicately etched with flowered patterns. It was filled with water, a lemon wedge
floating on the surface. After washing, she used that
fluffy towel, sighing at the softness of it. She'd never
felt a towel so lovely.

"I also had the restaurant cater the boys' meals today," Lucas said. "And the workers will get their fill.
Got to share a good thing."

Touched by his thoughtfulness, she came to the picnic
table, where he helped her onto the bench just as if they
were in a fancy restaurant and he was pulling out her
chair.

What was really going on? Was he kind of flirting,
just like yesterday? Or was this just an expression of
appreciation for showing him around today? Or maybe
he was hoping she'd brag about his kindness to reporters after he'd left?

All these questions she had. Couldn't he just make
a nice gesture without any cameras around and that
was that?

She decided that he was treating her out of the goodness of his heart. Just seeing how much he'd enjoyed
and been genuinely taken with Gabriel and the other
children yesterday told her that his gestures came from
a decent place.

Integrity, she thought. Even with Lucas's reputation,
she wanted to believe that he really did have it. In fact,
ever since her *abuelo* had told her the truth about her
father and mother—how Alicia was the product of a
sleazy one-night stand, how they had both deserted
her because neither of them had been responsible

enough to even raise a child—she'd searched for it. The possibility of finding some in a person like Lucas Chandler made her want to grab on, allowing it to pull her out from all the layers of mortification she was buried under.

He was taking a bottle of wine out of a basket. "Comte Armand, a wonderful burgundy."

"I don't—"

"Drink?" Shooting her a teasing grin, he tugged another bottle out of the ice bucket, deserting the more expensive wine. "Or there's always sparkling cider. I got it for variety."

Touched, Alicia fingered the flower vase in the middle of the table. "You think of everything."

"All your hard work deserves a treat."

He poured for her, then him, then opened a silver-lined cooler—a heater, really—and presented her with a basket of breads. She took one with cheese melted over the top while he poured oil and vinegar onto a side plate.

The cheese, tinted with garlic and herbs, made her close her eyes in pure pleasure.

Too decadent for her…usually. But why shouldn't she enjoy it while it lasted?

She opened her eyes to find him watching her. If she didn't know any better, she'd say he was taking as much happiness as she was out of her meal. Warmed by his interest, Alicia shivered.

He doled out the salad for her. "Want to know what surprised me yesterday, among other things?"

"I can't even begin to guess."

"That mojo you seem to have going with our friend

Gabe. He got pretty upset at the end of the day, but you seemed to know just how to handle him."

At Gabriel's name, Alicia pepped up. "From the day he came to the orphanage I've worked extra hard to win him over. He's come around, but you should've seen him before."

"Even more hyper?" Lucas hadn't said it unkindly at all. In fact, she suspected he had a tiny soft spot for Gabriel's vivacious spark, just as she did.

"He is active." She tossed her salad with a fork. "He always has been. But, at first he exhibited a mean streak, lashing out at the other children and the workers, throwing tantrums. He feels more comfortable now that he knows there are constant people in his life, thank goodness. And that's exactly what he needed—security. We don't know much about him except that he'd been abandoned by his parents so his trust is shaky."

A muscle flexed in his jaw, and she didn't have to be a mind reader to know that he was disturbed by the boy's background.

Welcome to life, she thought.

"You know," she added, "yesterday was a good day for him, but he still has his moments. We've had a part-time counselor who's seen him, so that helps, but in the long run he'll need a special family to give him a lot of attention and love."

A shot of panic seized her at the thought of him ever leaving. She'd become attached to the child and she knew it wasn't smart, but it'd just happened. He was charming and ultralovable; that was a part of his mercurial personality, though. He was a challenge her heart couldn't resist, because every time he needed reassurance or extra affection, she felt the responsibility to give it.

"I think," Lucas said, "we all need special families."

When he caught her understanding glance, he polished off his salad, not looking at her.

He seemed on the brink of saying something else, so she kept her tongue. A few seconds later, he laid down his fork, appearing so serious that she stopped eating.

"Have you ever thought—maybe one day when you're ready, I mean—of adopting? That's if you even want a family…"

He watched her intently.

"Yes." She hadn't even hesitated. If she could make sure a child like Gabriel grew up with people who adored him—people like her—she'd do it. Trouble was, everyone at Refugio Salvo thought the boy would be a tougher child to adopt out than most. He might always be passed over for the quieter ones and never even have the chance for a normal life out of the orphanage.

"I'd give anything to have a family again," she added.

"Your grandparents and parents…you miss them a lot. That's real obvious."

A pang of loss hit her square in the chest. He had no idea how much she wanted a group of people to surround her with love.

She blurted out her next heartfelt words before she even realized she'd said them. "Truthfully, all I want is a family. I even have dreams of children, especially the ones who are already born and need parents."

"That makes sense. I can see you and Gabriel together."

She had to fight a lump in her throat before she could answer. "Me, too. I can imagine that very clearly. But first, before any children, there's a husband...."

Silence emphasized the moan of wind through the branches as she concentrated on her food. Admitting her dreams out loud had made them all the more distant. For her, a family would also include a partner, because she believed in raising children the traditional two-parent way.

Too bad she couldn't adopt a man who would love her and bring back her dignity, too.

Avoiding any further revelations, she glanced at Lucas, who was considering her with a scrutiny that dug into her.

"And how about *you?*" she asked, returning the conversation to lightness. "Would Lucas Chandler, the big tycoon, ever consider adopting?"

At her question, he became even more intense, leaning on the table, his posture deceptively casual. "Only under the right circumstances."

Why did that sound as if he could mean so much more?

And why, Alicia asked herself with a growing mixture of trepidation and excitement, was she hoping he was back to flirting with her again?

Alicia took another bite of her salad instead of responding, but Lucas waited her out, using the opportunity to absorb her. She was wearing another prim, neat white blouse with short sleeves and crisp jeans to ride in.

The charms on her silver bracelet sang with her every move.

Anxiety throttled him again and he shifted on the bench. He still hadn't come to any conclusions about David's plan, but Lucas couldn't help feeling out Alicia, anyway. Why not? His desire to gain stature was probably going to force him into some kind of other PR relationship, anyway—he might as well admit it. He wanted the respect badly…so badly he could taste it.

So he filed away the information about her really, really wanting a family. She was a good woman who would make a good mother. Extra PR points for that—

He cut off the thought, disgusted with himself for even musing about it.

When Alicia finished her salad, Lucas brought out the next course, fettuccine slathered with a creamy marinara and topped with honey ricotta. Heaven.

She must've thought so, too, because the first bite caused her to do a little wiggly dance in her seat. Damn, it was cute.

"Know something?" he said. "I'm pretty surprised you're not giving me the hard sell about adopting one of the boys now, like a spokeswoman usually would. I get the feeling you'd normally never let this chance go with anyone else who'd visit the property."

"It shouldn't be a pressured decision, Mr…Lucas." She smiled. "If adopting was in your heart, then you won't need to be talked into making it happen."

Ouch. But he recovered because he had to. "I think you just know when to let something lie."

She took a sip of her sparkling cider, then slowly put

it down. "My grandparents taught me how to do that. They were full of good advice and lessons to learn from."

Lucas thought about his own family. He'd learned by example from them, too, except it was to do the *opposite* of whatever his dad did.

"We weren't very well off," she added, "but my grandparents scraped up enough money to give me a great home and an education. I realized from them what was important in life—the basics. And they showed me it was necessary to be thankful for every one of them."

"College." He was genuinely interested to hear more about her. "Where did you go?"

"Oh, just a community school. And it turned out that it wasn't for me. So I decided to work as a receptionist and contribute to the household, just as I did when I worked waitressing jobs in high school until I knew what I wanted. But eventually my *abuelo* died."

A shadow seemed to pass over her face as she returned to eating.

She hadn't explained anything, really, had she?

"And how did *you* become the philanthropist you are today?" she asked, clearly changing the subject.

"Oh, you know…" He twirled some noodles onto his fork. "The usual rich-kid tales. The best schools, the best of everything. My mom divorced me and my dad when I was real young. She decided life as a socialite was too empty and she took off for parts unknown to take advantage of her anthropology degree, doing lots of fieldwork, from what I understand."

"You don't talk to her?"

"Occasionally." When Lucas took a bite, the food was suddenly tasteless. "She attempts to make contact from each of her research locations but, more often than not, she's in a village with no modern technology and bad cell-phone reception."

"So you don't know her very well." Alicia's soft gaze was sympathetic.

"Right. But that's okay. I've had a lot of stepmoms to take her place. Four, by my last count."

"*Four?* Are you close to any of them?"

"Nope. I did get a half brother out of the deal, though. Luckily, he's the only other child my dad bothered to have. Unleashing two cynical Chandler boys into society is enough."

"Cynical." Alicia laughed. "You?"

She wasn't being sarcastic. Not this straightforward woman who barely knew him. It was a nice change of pace for once.

"I'm afraid so. See, we were raised by a man who values cold, hard success above everything."

Alicia tipped her glass to her mouth, the rim resting against her bottom lip. Lucas found himself leaning closer, envying the glass.

She finally took another sip, ending his reverie.

"So, am I to think that your father soured you on marriage?"

Her words were a punch to the gut.

He swallowed, nerves screaming. "In the past, I thought I might avoid getting hitched. I didn't want to be a serial husband like my dad."

"And that's why you…" She gently swished around

her glass, seeking words, the cider spinning around like a liquid golden web.

"I what?" He wanted to hear her say it.

She smiled sweetly and his heart flipped.

"That's why you date all those women," she said. "At least, that's what they say."

Yeah, all *those* women. The ones who didn't have any interest in families at all. There was a cold comfort in that kind of emptiness. Security. And the more Lucas thought about David's suggestion that he find an "appropriate" woman, the more he came to believe that it wouldn't be much of a change from his previous relationships. He wouldn't *have* to invest emotion. It was a business deal, pure and simple. A situation that would benefit everyone all around. His girlfriend could spend his money any way she wanted to, especially when it came to taking part in charity work that would generate positive ink in the press. And Lucas would be a better man—at least in the eyes of the world.

Putting down her glass, Alicia then propped her elbows on the table and rested her chin on her palms. She was just as beautiful as David had said, even more so. Her physical appearance whipped his overused libido into a frenzy, but that's not what really tore Lucas up about her.

She had soul. A sincerity you had to travel far and wide to find. Something he'd never experienced.

"You want to know the truth?" he asked.

"What?"

Lucas pushed his plate away, appetite for food gone. So many other appetites stoked.

"I wouldn't mind finding a wife at all. Someday."

Her eyes had gotten a little wider, probably because his comment clashed with his reputation.

Before he knew it, he found himself laying the groundwork to take the next step in this plan—not that he was going to go further. Hell, no, he was still thinking about all the pros and cons. He wanted to measure the possibilities, that's all.

Measure *her* to see if she'd be a fit….

"I know you're doing your best to save the world in this small corner of the earth," he said, pulse picking up speed, "but what if you had the chance to make changes on a large scale? How far would you go to get that opportunity?"

She was getting curious about where he was leading. He could tell from her puzzled smile.

"How big of an opportunity are we talking about?" she asked.

"Getting loads of money to spend as you see fit, on any cause that would speak to you."

Her lips parted, her eyes going hazy, her head tilting.

He fought himself, feeling his inner playboy stir: The guy who loved fine champagne and loud music. The guy who loved a good, dirty, heart-stopping off-road race in expensive mechanical toys.

The guy who'd surprisingly been struck with respect for this woman's apparent selflessness.

"I would do just about anything to get that kind of chance," she said, her voice almost a whisper.

Anything, he thought. Would she even sign on for a fake liaison with a billionaire? Somehow he doubted it. A person with such devotion to others would never hop into such a calculating situation and compromise herself like that.

So why was he even pursuing this subject?

The images overtook him again. A woman who would bring grace and charity to his name.

"But," she said in a dismissive tone, "this is just a hypothetical question, so why think too hard about it? I'll never see that sort of opportunity."

Something about the way she concentrated on eating her salad again made Lucas wonder how much she really did long for the chance.

And if she was worth the extra effort it would take to secure himself a perfect partner.

Chapter Four

Over the next few days Lucas found himself taking every opportunity to be near Alicia, whether it was at the orphanage where he just "spontaneously" showed up for arts-and-crafts hour with the boys or even at mealtime, when he could sit with her and enjoy another conversation.

Even as he still mulled over David's suggestion, he found that he genuinely couldn't get enough of this woman—her sincerity, her genuine interest as they talked about everything from the places he'd traveled to the scrapbooking she liked to do as a hobby. He also found out that she was a history buff and that, if she watched TV at all, it was to tune in to programs about California's evolution or even World War II, which her grandfather had been a veteran of. That made him remember his own deceased granddad; somewhere along the line Lucas had heard that he, too, had been a soldier, but in the Pacific theater, not the European one. It bothered him that he didn't know more.

And then there was Gabe, who, for some reason, always made a beeline for Lucas. Maybe it was because Lucas tended to sneak those chocolates from his hotel pillow out of the room and into the kid's waiting hand while no one was looking. Or maybe it was because Lucas couldn't help laughing with the boy as he rocketed around the dining area or the playground.

Or…God, maybe Lucas merely liked to sit there and get lost in the sight of Alicia hugging Gabe just when it looked as if he really needed it. Maybe that was what kept Lucas coming back, because he could see how happy it made the kid.

He could imagine what it would've been like if he'd only had someone around who'd cared enough to do the same for him, once upon a time.

During these visits, only two reporters had lingered, and they were both from TCO-owned papers. Lucas supposed the rest had left because he wasn't providing much in the way of encouraging salacious copy that would sell news. But, at least, he was making headway with this whole "rebirth of his reputation" deal, and that's what mattered.

Yet, it did occur to him that he could be making even more if he could just decide whether or not to pursue this crazy idea….

An instantly respectable man, he thought as he buttoned himself into a pressed linen shirt that felt like a coffin. Outside his window here at the renowned Playa de Realeza resort, the surf beat against the rocks. Each forceful pound worked at him, pushed him further back into a stifling hole.

There was a knock at his door and, when Lucas moved to open it, he found David.

"Dressed to thrill?" his brother asked, stepping into the room as Lucas closed the door behind him. He was garbed in the usual polished suit. The way it balanced on his frame, as if he'd been born to wear expensive threads, unnerved Lucas. "Or am I wrong about what you've been doing these past few days?"

"I've been doing what I've agreed to—getting good publicity."

"Sure. Right. It's got everything to do with that."

Without invitation, David made himself comfortable on a dark leather couch. Around him, the glass-topped table, original modern art and designer furniture all seemed excessive and totally unnecessary when Lucas thought about what Refugio Salvo needed but didn't have.

"Good PR is what we've been getting, though," David added, referring to the positive stories that had, indeed, hit the papers because of this trip. "But, in case you don't remember, I need to get back to New York tonight for a board meeting tomorrow, so vacation's over. As it is, we've overstayed."

At the notion of leaving, something rebelled inside Lucas, clamping inside his stomach.

Noticing Lucas's hesitation, David sat up, a slow smile spreading over his mouth. "I knew it."

"What're you talking about?"

"You don't want to go anywhere."

Lucas turned away from David, suddenly in search of the tie he hadn't planned on wearing or even a jacket he wouldn't need out in the nice weather—anything to make his brother think he was on the wrong track. "If I needed to be anyplace else, I'd go. But where would that be?"

David shrugged, acknowledging that Lucas had a token office that had been visited by its occupant maybe three times in all these years. And there was no question that Lucas couldn't be traipsing around the globe making headlines again.

So where *did* he belong right now? Where did he have to be if not here?

"Whether you admit it or not," David said, "I know what you're trying to do." He laughed. "So my idea wasn't so ridiculous, after all, huh? What made you change your mind?"

Alicia, laughing at his jokes and spending time with him, making him feel as if she didn't want to be anyplace else but here, either, especially with little Gabe pulling Lucas toward the playground and spouting cute nonsense like, "Come on! Let's go! Monkey boy, monkey boy."

"Who says I've changed my mind?" he ground out.

"Spare me." On his feet now, the CEO started pacing, arms crossed as he shifted into genius mode. "Does she have any inkling?"

"Of course not, because I'm not going to do it."

Bull, said the rusty angel on his shoulder whom he'd

never paid much attention to in the past. *Your nose is gonna hit the wall if you don't stop lying to yourself.*

David obviously agreed with the old conscience, because he ignored Lucas's refusal altogether. "If I were you, Luke, I wouldn't breathe a word of this—what should we call it?—*relationship of convenience* to her. With a little more work, you've got her. I've seen the way she looks at you when you're not aware of it."

A flash of desire lit through Lucas at this proof of Alicia's reluctant attraction. Sure, he'd suspected her interest, but she was so damned stuck on avoiding it that he'd almost talked himself into thinking he was wrong.

As he dwelled on the fantasy of it, a slow thaw ran down his body, just under the skin. It heated him up as he imagined catching her in one of those looks someday.

Still, Lucas kept his head on straight. "It's a long way from secret looks to a commitment."

"I give up." David walked toward the door. "If she's going to be so hard to win over, let's go another way. I can set something up with another decent candidate within the week."

Someone Lucas actually enjoyed being with?

Or, more importantly, someone who made him feel as if he was a decent guy for the first time in his life?

"If I'm going to dive into this situation," Lucas said, "it might as well be with a woman I like."

But his conscience was gnawing at him again, yet in a different way. How could he even think of fooling her into this?

Just concentrate on the longing in her gaze when you

asked her about doing charity work on a more wide-spread basis, his other side argued. *Just remember how happy you could make her with your money.*

Coming back to the moment, Lucas realized that David was still in the room. As a matter of fact, he was even staring at Lucas with a new respect.

"You'd really do this for TCO?" David asked.

Chest tightening with some kind of emotion that could've been either good *or* bad, Lucas reluctantly nodded.

"I was wrong, then," the other man said. "You just might be a man to be reckoned with, after all. Dad's going to be impressed."

The magic words. Ones that almost erased Lucas's misgivings.

But not quite.

"Ready…" Alicia shouted, her voice echoing against the sky as she poised the Wiffle ball to throw it. "And…go!"

She tossed the sphere into the air, where a crowd of overeager little boys raised their hands to clumsily catch it. The light ball sailed over Gabriel's head and, with a squeal, he turned around to Juan, a five-year-old who'd batted it down to the grass and was diving on top of it. Immersed in the fun, Gabriel fell on Juan while the other boys followed suit, piling on top of each other like puppies.

The younger boys were in the middle of playtime while the older children attended class in the school building, taught by nuns who were proficient in their chosen subjects. On the sidelines of this little game, Sister Elisabeth sat in a lawn chair, her long skirt spread around her as she crocheted. Her chubby cheeks glowed while she smiled at the children's exuberance.

"Whoa, there, young fellers," Lucas called out, jogging over to the pile and playfully helping Juan out of the mess of little-kid limbs. "Poor Juan's gotta breathe."

Laughing, Alicia watched as the billionaire set the five-year-old on his feet and mussed his hair. He was having as much fun as the children, distinguished from them only by his height, heft and expensive clothing. Where they were garbed in their modest T-shirts and jeans, he was wearing top-of-the-line pants and a fine button-down shirt.

It didn't seem right, she thought. Lucas Chandler was better suited to a more relaxed wardrobe. Yes, he'd loosened his collar and rolled up his sleeves, but she intuitively knew that this wasn't how he liked to dress. It was in the ruffled cut of his hair, the no-holds-barred joy of his laugh when he allowed himself to cut loose, as he was doing now.

Once again she felt the connection that had tugged at her right from the very start—an invisible line that seemed to draw some kind of understanding between them.

As she ran a hungry gaze over him, she caught herself.

Not before you get married, Alicia. You shouldn't even be thinking about it unless he were to get down on his knees and beg you to be his wife.

As if that would ever happen.

She shook her head. Billionaires fell for antiflashy

home-and-hearth women like her all the time. She'd be a real asset to his lifestyle, wouldn't she?

"Heads up!" she heard him yell.

The impact of his voice on her body made her jerk to attention. As the ball spun through the sunshine, his tone melted through her like a physical thing, like a caress of heat through her bones.

The ball plopped onto the grass five feet away, inviting all the small boys to run for it.

With an excited "Eek!" Alicia joined in, pretending she was racing for the prize, too.

Gabriel, the most determined of anyone, snatched the sphere and held it to his chest. "Nice ball!" he shouted, laughing.

She applauded him, loving his obvious enjoyment. Gabriel seemed to require more validation than most, and once again, she wondered what kind of parents he'd had, how long it would take for him to get over their desertion.

He was already on his feet, throwing the ball. It was a good effort for a three-year-old, awkward but not without potential.

"Look at that arm," Lucas said, bending to his knees so he could retrieve the Wiffle from the ground. "I see major league in this kid's future."

He looked just as proud as Gabriel did, and Alicia's heart wrapped around the sight. Whether the playboy would admit it or not, he was meant to be a father. Every second around these orphans, especially Gabriel, proved it. There was something in his eyes that she didn't see when he was doing anything else, like posing for pictures or riding a horse around the property. Something she wanted to touch and absorb.

As Lucas grinned at the child, something primal flickered within her—the recognition of a protector. Her body grew warm, as if a furnace had been stoked and lit. The heat grew sexual, spreading between her legs and twisting there like a writhing flame.

And, a little higher up, she felt the slow ache of desire.

Lucas rose to his full height, holding the ball and enthusiastically glancing at Alicia. But when he saw how she was staring at him—probably with clear appreciation written all over her face—his smile faltered and he grew more serious.

As their gazes connected, a glass world seemed to shatter between them.

"Throw!" one little boy yelled. "Throw!"

The other children joined in the chorus, pulling Alicia out of her stupor. Blushing at what had passed between her and the billionaire—a moment that had been repeated over and over with every one of his visits—she got back into the game, desperate to ignore the lure of him.

"Throw!" Alicia chanted with the boys, clapping her hands and becoming the distant hostess yet again. "Throw, throw…"

For a second, Lucas squeezed the plastic ball as if to throttle it. Brow knitted, he glanced down at the toy as if it held some kind of answer to whatever he was asking himself.

Are you wondering how sad I'll be when you leave?

she mused. *Because now that I've met you, I think I'm going to miss having you around.*

He excited her, made her realize that in many ways she'd been sleepwalking through life—until he'd shown up.

This was not necessarily a positive thing, either, because she didn't want to feel, didn't want to *need* a man who had no use for her in his high-flying life.

Gabriel began to jump up and down in front of Lucas and his frown morphed into a grin. At that moment, Alicia would've sworn that the little boy could talk the man into anything.

As if realizing it, too, he winked at Gabriel, then lightly tossed the ball while shouting, "Up for grabs!"

Alicia got into the action, teasing the crowd by saying, "I'm gonna get it, I've got it, I've—"

Gabriel pounced on the ball again. But now he imitated *Sesame Street*'s Bert doing The Pigeon, victoriously kicking out his leg in a weirdly endearing dance he'd learned during TV time.

What a boy.

Ending his display, Gabriel threw the ball, and Alicia caught it. The kids applauded her, just as she always did for them.

"Thank you." She made a tiny curtsy.

Out of the corner of her eye she saw Lucas run a hand over his mouth to cover a laugh, and a flash of goose bumps covered her skin.

Great, more lust.

She threw the ball, but in her determination to chase

away the sensations, her focus and, thus, her aim were slightly off.

The Wiffle bonked Lucas right in the *cabeza*.

The billionaire merely blinked his eyes in reaction as the ball thudded to the grass. He stared at it on the ground, a vengeful expression spreading over his face.

Oh-oh.

In the meantime, the boys had descended on the ball. Someone threw it again and the game went on.

But Lucas just stood there as he slid his gaze to her.

Her heartbeat began jackhammering.

"Sorry?" she said.

He shook his head slowly. The gesture was so steeped in the promise of something more adult than a Wiffle-ball game that the blood kicked through her veins.

As his gaze narrowed, Alicia's adrenaline took over. *Run,* she thought. *Run for your…what?*

Chastity? Life?

With a burst of giggling panic, she moved back an inch, then yelled, "Sister Elisabeth!" in an attempt to recruit a defender.

When she sent the nun a pleading look, she saw that the lady was giving her a This-is-your-business glance. Then she returned her attention to the boys, who were playing ball very nicely on their own. No help there.

Lucas angled his body toward her. "Was nailing me your way of getting my attention?"

She swallowed, her heart flittering. She offered a sweet smile and a shrug in answer.

"Because," he continued, taking a predatory step closer, "you don't have to work that hard for it."

At his frank comment, she stumbled back another step. But all that did was encourage him. Something flashed in his gaze, and she knew she'd better start running.

From more than just his teasing, too.

With a yelp, she gathered her midshin-length skirt and took off, heading toward a nearby hill and hoping he'd lose interest before she got there. The oxygen was thin and sharp in her lungs and she held back a girlish squeak at the thought of getting caught.

Nearer, nearer, almost there...

She didn't want to look back, even if seeing him was all she'd been craving. No, instead, she pumped her arms, laughing wildly as she crested the hill and began the descent.

But when her skirt tangled with her legs, she lost it, stumbling, reaching out her arms as the grass rushed up toward her.

"Whoa!" It was Lucas's voice, right at her back.

Before she could smack the ground, she felt his thick arm around her waist, flipping her over, her back to his front as he took the brunt of the fall.

They rolled to a stop, panting, the sun shining down on her face.

For a short eternity, she felt every muscle of his chest, his stomach, his legs against her. Something wicked and buried noticed how well they fit together with her rear end nestled against him.

Spooning, she thought, recalling how her high-school friends and her coworkers in San Diego had talked at lunchtime.

Breathless, she closed her eyes, feeling his chest rise and fall against her back, feeling his arm tightening around her.

Her belly flared with forbidden heat again, prickling the areas around it. Wanting him, needing him…

She felt his breath on her hair. His hand rested on her stomach, fingers splayed and infusing her with trembling desire.

One minute, she thought. Couldn't she enjoy this for one minute and then go back to her personal vows of celibacy?

Forgetting herself—oh, that's all she wanted to do—Alicia slowly turned her head, shifting ever so slightly to open her eyes and glance up at him.

His lips were right there, so close, so tempting…

Don't do it.

But she couldn't stop, not when she'd been fantasizing about this for a string of long nights.

With tentative wonder, she brushed her mouth over his.

It was as if a shock of raw static had fizzed through her, ripping her apart at every joint. She buzzed with the feel of him, filled herself with his scent and the scratch of whisker friction against her face.

Relaxed and tense all at the same time, she opened her mouth a little more, their lips fully connecting, warm breath mingling and moist. His arm pressed into her, his fingers digging into her stomach as if to draw her out of the mental shelter she'd hidden herself in.

More, she thought, dizzy and restless.

She wanted so much more.

But the sound of a child's voice in the near distance shook her to reality. Then other voices joined the first as laughter danced on the air.

Horrified, Alicia broke away from Lucas, too afraid to look at him to see what his reaction might be. Her heartbeat rumbled like rocks falling down a mountain.

Lord, what had she done?

She didn't have time to answer, because the boys were upon them before she could fully scoot away from the man she'd just thrown herself at.

"Miss Alicia!" they cried, crashing into her and hugging her against them as if she were the Wiffle ball now.

"Hey, hey!" she heard Lucas saying as he was overwhelmed by them, too.

One of the better English speakers, Miguel, said, "Where you go, Miss Alicia?"

At that moment, Juan smothered her with an embrace, so she couldn't answer, thank goodness.

Then she heard Gabriel's voice. "No! Off, off!"

Suddenly Juan was blindsided by Gabriel, and Alicia sucked in a stunned breath. He was in one of his moods; you couldn't predict when they would happen, but obviously Juan's affection had triggered the boy's jealousy.

Gabriel screamed, tears gushing down his face while he held Juan in a clumsy headlock. The older child sent Alicia a helpless glance while pulling at Gabriel's arms. He'd been taught not to hurt the younger children.

"Stop it, Gabriel!"

But before she could physically intervene, Lucas

was there, separating the two. Freed, Juan scuttled away, distancing himself from trouble. That left Gabriel with his fists bunched, his face red as he kicked at the ground.

"Hey, there's no reason for this," Lucas said, tone firm yet gentle.

The boy raised his fists as if to strike out.

"Gabe."

At Lucas's voice, the boy stopped, fighting his tears and watching the man to see what he would do from here.

Alicia held her breath.

When Lucas tentatively rested a hand on Gabriel's head, the child began to cry again, sending the billionaire a heartbreaking look that Alicia translated as a plea to understand his frustration.

In response, Lucas merely stroked the boy's hair, his gaze going soft.

Weren't playboys supposed to run away at this point? she wondered, her throat stinging.

Sister Elisabeth appeared at the top of the hill. "Boys…"

Her voice was quiet, stern, tolerating no defiance. They all came to her within seconds, and she led them away with a backward sympathetic glance at Alicia. She was trusting her to deal with Gabriel, as most of the nuns always did.

Sometimes she wondered how Gabriel would fare if she weren't around to handle him.

As if to validate her concern, the boy turned his tear-streaked face to her.

"I'm still here," she said. "Don't worry, Gabriel."

Then she went to him, gathering him in her arms. Yet he also reached out to Lucas, holding the man's hand as if anchoring himself on both sides.

"Man," the child said between tears.

That must've been Gabriel's way of asking if Lucas would be around for a longer time, too. She glanced up at him, wondering the same thing.

How long will you be here?

At Lucas's troubled gaze, Alicia couldn't even begin to guess the answer. Instead, she started to shiver again.

Just as she did whenever he looked at her.

Chapter Five

An hour later, Alicia was still trying to pretend the kiss hadn't happened.

While she, Lucas and Sister Elisabeth had escorted the children inside for "quiet time," Alicia had done her best to find every distraction available, to busy herself with anything but Lucas and the puzzling emotions he stirred up in her. She'd lavished attention on the boys as they'd all shuffled off to their rooms. Then, when the Sister had mentioned that a two-year-old they called Jaime was a little fussy, Alicia had eagerly volunteered to lull him to sleep while Lucas and Sister Elisabeth took care of the others.

It'd granted her some time alone, an escape that was allowing her to get her head together.

Now she rocked Jaime and sang him a lullaby. The air in the family room, with its silent television, walls of books and neatly stowed games, was laced with peace, as well as the spices used for the chicken mole they would be having for dinner.

A clear head, she thought, watching the boy in her arms as he breathed in serenity. *I can finally think rationally again.*

Alicia didn't know how long she felt that way before sensing Lucas's presence and glancing up to find him.

He stood in the doorway, concentrating on the child in her arms, an odd look on his face.

Her starved libido seized the opportunity to secretly watch him; her body recognized the broad shoulders, the violet-hued eyes from all the dreams she'd tried to stifle at night. Yet, even during this battle to be immune to him, the last notes of her lullaby misted away as her mouth went dry.

When her gaze refocused itself, she discovered that he was visually devouring her, too. She'd been caught.

Time seemed to spin and change shape, confusing the minutes into what seemed like hours. In the taut void, she allowed him to enter her in some inexplicable way, warming her with all their unspoken words.

If I just gave him permission, she thought, *if I moved just an inch or said yes, even silently, he would know how much he tempts me, how much I want him.*

But that was impossible.

She heard her ailing *abuelo*'s final words once again as he lay pale in the hospital bed.

"Before it's too late," he'd said, "I must confess something to you, *mija*."

And, just like that, he'd unburdened himself of all the lies she'd lived under her entire life. Lies that had once covered her with security, like the one she'd been told about how her parents had died in a car accident.

The truth had been more than ugly.

Before she'd been born, her *abuelo* had said, Alicia's untamable father had moved down to Mexico after a terrible family fight. There he'd believed he could live cheaply and freely.

It'd broken their hearts to let him go, yet Alicia's father, Edgar, refused to change and his parents wouldn't tolerate his wild habits. They were at an impasse.

"We didn't know this," *Abuelo* had added, holding her hand weakly, "but Edgar fell on hard times and began to earn money by…" Here, he'd choked to a stop as Alicia sat in her bedside chair, frozen by what she was hearing.

Then he'd mustered some strength, finishing his sentence while watching Alicia with pity. "By servicing wealthy women at the resorts in order to earn his way."

That was when Alicia, strictly raised and sheltered, had floated out of body, listening to what must be a stranger's story. That's what she'd kept telling herself, anyway.

Her *abuelo* had continued relieving his soul, confessing how Edgar had accidentally impregnated an early forties, unmarried one-night stand. As a Catholic, the woman had decided to repent after she'd found out about the baby; she'd refused to terminate the pregnancy but had no problem talking a guilt-ridden, easily influenced Edgar into accepting the child after she'd given birth. Knowing the single, divorced mother wanted nothing to do with Alicia, especially since she'd refused custody of her other children, he'd turned to his parents, feeling too guilty to give his child up for adoption before he could beg his mama and papa to take the baby into their home.

They'd loved Alicia right away, *Abuelo* had said, and promised to help their son raise her. But they had one condition for him: that he change his ways and be a good father.

But it was too much to ask because, after two months, he'd buckled under the responsibility. On the day he ran away, he'd left only two things: his baby, plus a silver charm bracelet as a wish for his daughter to someday remember her papa.

All her life, her grandparents had claimed that her dead father had intended to give the jewelry to Alicia himself at her *Quinceanera,* a fifteenth-birthday celebration. But that had obviously been a lie, too.

Her father had never planned to come back at all.

Rocked by shame at these revelations, she'd buried the shocking truth while tending to her sick *abuelo,* who ultimately succumbed to his pneumonia by nightfall. But something had altered her self-perception. She didn't know who she was, anymore, aside from the fact that she'd been born out of sin.

In the fallout, the only thing she could think to do was mindlessly quit her job, sell the home she couldn't bear to stay in anymore since it reminded her of how she'd gotten there in the first place, then seek answers. Any answers.

Desperation had led her to Rosarito Beach's resorts, where her parents had met, but her journey had been a futile one. Neither her father nor her mother could be accounted for, leaving her with so many questions and fears about who they were and what kind of legacy they'd left her.

In the end, unable to track anyone or anything down, she'd felt lonelier than ever, wishing for her grandparents, for a home. She missed the stability of her old life.

Missed the comforting lies that had kept her emotionally safe for years.

And, yet, it was then she found her true path. While struggling with her turmoil, she'd experimentally attended mass near Rosarito, drawn by the comforting pageantry of the Catholic church and thinking their old rituals might hold some answer she hadn't discovered yet. That's when she'd talked to Sister Elisabeth and found some purpose during their casual chats. She'd clung to the idea of finding solace in charity and redeeming herself through kind deeds.

The encounters had also made her realize that her parents' story was even more reason to uphold the personal chastity vow she'd already made after losing her virginity. It was a balm, a way to make up for the bone-deep disgust at the sinful choices her parents had made. Publicly she could also convince everyone that she really was a decent person, no matter what her parents had been and no matter what she'd done by following in their footsteps with that teenage boy.

She'd grown up in a house of morals and had always been told by her grandparents that she was good. To lose that identity and admit that she was just like her actual parents was unthinkable….

Disturbed by the mere thought of it, Alicia pulled her gaze away from the intense promise of Lucas Chandler, steadying herself until her heart began thudding in regular cadence again. As she held tighter to the boy in her arms, the silver heart charms on her bracelet brushed the child's skin. Like a penance, the jewelry always served to remind her of why she'd left San Diego, clasping her wrist with the weight of what she needed to conquer.

As if thrown off balance, Lucas cleared his throat softly, then moved toward a timeworn couch to take a seat.

The situation felt oddly innocent, with the famous playboy sitting across a room just as if he were paying a harmless call on her, so she didn't run away as she probably should have.

But that made no sense. He had much more to accomplish here than dally with her. Even though there were no cameras around today, she knew he was at Refugio Salvo for business and no other reason.

He cleared his throat again, and she risked a friendly, hopefully neutral, smile at him, testing to see if that would get her back on track. And it did, thank goodness. Saved.

"You look so natural like that," he whispered, nodding at Jaime cuddled against her.

"When the time is right, it'll be even more natural." She laid her cheek against Jaime's head, listening to him breathe against her.

"And when will the right time be?"

His question was so direct that she almost stopped rocking in her chair.

Noticing her obvious discomfort, he whispered, "Sorry. I guess I'm too curious about you."

His gaze lasered into her, and she grasped for control once again. Why was he so interested in this stuff, anyway?

He took a breath, leaned forward in his seat, then braced his arms on his thighs. He seemed so focused that Alicia actually held on to Jaime a little tighter.

"I guess I'm just wondering how long it actually takes to realize it's the right time with someone," he said. "Does it happen after a month? A week?"

Yes, how long *should* it take?

As if in a dream, she saw herself pressed against Lucas Chandler, lifting her face to him as he bent down to fit his lips against hers. She imagined how powerful more of his kisses would be, how persuasive and deep, bringing back all the passion she'd repressed for so many years....

No. Lucas Chandler was the last person she should be trusting in this area.

But he wasn't necessarily talking about sex here, was he? It sounded more as though he was referring to love.

Why? What kind of possible interest could he have in that?

"I guess," she said softly, "I'll know when I know."

Unless she already did know....

Again, she stopped herself. The thought was too

rash—and hadn't that gotten her and her parents into trouble before?

Lucas pushed out a heavy breath, in his thinker's pose again. "Sometimes, I think you just *know*, even right away, what you need in your life. I'm not convinced it takes a lot of dithering around to be sure once you've found it."

The room seemed to be compressing against her. What was he talking about? She couldn't understand….

"Alicia…" He scooted forward a little. "I'm going to be leaving soon, you know—"

It was at that moment she realized that they weren't alone.

Thank goodness they weren't alone.

"Gabriel?" She spied him standing in the entry. Then she switched to Spanish. "What are you doing out of your room?"

His cheeks were flushed, his hair bed-headed. "The man." He turned to the billionaire as if he had Lucas radar and was helpless in its powers.

But, much to her surprise, Lucas seemed to have something pretty similar, too. He was already out of his seat, kneeling in front of the child. "I thought I'd hang around and bother Miss Alicia. What's your excuse?"

At the way he so easily interacted with Gabriel, Alicia ached. It was overwhelming seeing this supposedly fly-by-night man showing such care for the orphan who clearly worshipped him.

In response, Gabriel held up his arms, and, without pause, Lucas scooped him up. As if it were perfectly natural, the boy leaned his head on the man's shoulder and closed his eyes.

Touched, Alicia couldn't stop the images from suffusing her mind: Lucas holding Gabriel like this, in sickness and in health, every day. Lucas raising the orphan as his own child, providing him with all he would ever need, such as enough clothing, food, guidance, a college education.

Then, shockingly, she saw herself entering the fantasy's frame, walking up to Lucas and Gabriel to join the family picture.

Somewhere to belong, she thought.

But reality ripped the image apart. Instead, she realized that she was sitting across the room from the other two, removed and left behind.

"What a team," she said, nodding at them, wishing she could be a part of it.

Even though Lucas didn't say anything, his glance seemed to speak volumes.

Maybe we could be, it said. *Maybe we could be a great team.*

But maybe it was all in her starved imagination.

Lucas and Alicia managed to slip Gabe and Jaime into their beds before either boy woke up again. Yet, as soon as Gabe left Lucas's arms, the tycoon felt a little emptier than when he'd first walked into the orphanage today.

He couldn't pinpoint why. He didn't want to. All he knew was that Alicia *was* attracted to him.

Back in the family room, when he'd first picked up Gabe, Lucas had felt as if something had clicked into place, as if he'd found a part of himself that'd been missing, like a gear that helped a machine work properly. But, with Gabe snuggling up to him like that, it'd been easy to fool himself. And, when the kid had fallen back asleep right away, Lucas had even found it simple to believe that he had some sort of touch with him, just like Alicia.

That he could actually matter in someone's life.

As he'd held the kid, he hadn't needed his brother around to catch Alicia's surreptitious admiration. In a bared moment, he'd seen one of those looks she'd been keeping a secret: a soft longing in her gaze, a slight parting of her lips.

It'd taken all of his strength to keep from going to her and revealing everything.

Just come with me, he'd wanted to say. *We can have a good thing. We can make each other happy, even if it's all business.*

But…couldn't it be more? Especially after that kiss she'd given him earlier? Especially after the touch of her mouth on his had almost drilled him into the ground with an intensity he'd never felt before?

As he shut the door to Gabe's room and joined Alicia in the hallway, he told himself that he was very wrong. That he needed respect more than any kind of affection.

On track again, he reminded himself that this woman needed to be won over with emotion, not promises of luxury.

"I think Gabriel is really asleep this time," Alicia said.

Lucas saw the willingness written in her relaxed

posture, in the way she wasn't stepping away from him to create a polite boundary this time. No, his care with Gabe had changed something about the way she was receiving him now. Hell, after that kiss earlier, she'd barely been able to even look at him.

At the end of his limits, he deliberately reached out, not knowing exactly where he wanted to touch, just knowing he wanted to feel her skin under his fingertips.

But when her eyes widened, he reconsidered, changed tack and smoothed back a curl from her face. Yet he did it with deliberation, wallowing in the contact.

It was as if the air had gone dark, an exploded light that had robbed the room of illumination while providing way too much of it at the same time. A buzz of electric hunger zapped up his fingers, his arm, blasting through the rest of his body and making him realize how damned far he'd go to touch her again.

As she sucked in a breath, he kept his hand where it was, daring her to inch away this time, daring her to deny what she felt for him. He needed her to want him for so many reasons.

But what he especially needed, he told himself stridently, was for her to fall quickly for him.

When she stayed where she was, eyes hazed over with pure, unadulterated desire, Lucas's groin tightened.

Mine, he thought. *I want you to be mine.*

"What're you doing tonight?" he asked, voice graveled.

"I…"

"I want you to come to dinner with me at the resort. They have one of the best restaurants in the country."

"Lucas…" She seemed to sway toward him.

His fingers burrowed deeper into her thick hair.

Don't back away. Please don't.

But then she inhaled, as if coming to her senses. With a swallow, she straightened her spine then tucked back the strand of hair he'd caressed. For good measure, she ran her hands over her skirt as if she needed something else to do.

"I can't meet you for dinner or…anything," she said.

The bottom fell out from under him. She couldn't? He wasn't used to hearing that. But he donned a smile all the same, allowing the Dimples to cover his sharp disappointment.

"I understand."

She laughed civilly, touching her bracelet without seeming to realize she was doing it again. Nervous habit, he supposed.

"You do?" she asked.

"Sure. By now you've probably heard about all my colorful adventures in detail, so you're afraid that more than your reputation will get smashed to smithereens."

"Rumors don't matter. You've done—"

"I know. I've done so much for the orphanage. You still don't know the details about Cecilia DuPont? Or any of the others?"

She shook her head.

God, why was he going there with the gossip? Did he *want* her to start watching him with higher-than-thou judgment? Was he searching for a reason that would explain her rejection? Or maybe he was just ruining this callous plan before it could come to fruition.

"I'll have to show you the photos sometime," he said. "The reporters got a real good one of Cecilia with her dress—"

"Stop, Lucas."

His stomach was coiled so tightly he thought he'd explode. "You don't want to know?"

"I don't have to." She sighed, then gave him a shatteringly genuine look. "I think there's much more to you than those pictures could ever say."

He was still waiting for her to realize how wrong she was and, perhaps, to validate all the disgust he held for himself.

Couldn't she see the truth?

"Just..." Alicia shook her head. "Just believe me when I tell you that any more time with you alone is more than I can handle. There. I said it. And...please don't ask me to explain, because I won't."

She was nervous about something, but... God, she'd kissed him earlier.

Kissed *him.*

And...he had to get this straight. She was rejecting him because of *herself?* Now he really didn't understand. But, all the same, he wanted to respect her wishes. No one had ever made him feel that he could someday be better than what the press said he was and he didn't want to ruin that by forcing the issue and proving all the skeptics right.

So where did that leave him?

In the dust, he thought as Alicia quietly moved away from him, down the hall and out of his range.

Yup, he thought. Alone again and in the dust.

As he went the opposite way, toward an exit, he didn't know what to do next.

But he didn't have to wonder for long, because that's when word of the fire at an orphanage down the coast hit.

And his own problems didn't matter, anymore.

Chapter Six

Alicia would never forget the moment Guillermo Ramos caught her near the kitchen and urgently whispered the news about the fire, because it had been the prelude to the rest of her life.

The administrator had quietly yet efficiently spread the news to all the other employees, throwing Refugio Salvo into a contained frenzy. Taking care not to upset the napping younger children, the adults and older orphans sprang into action, preparing to accept the boys from a devastated orphanage miles away.

A fire had consumed that property and, although there'd been no deaths, there was so much damage that the children had to be parceled out to existing sites, even if the other orphanages didn't have the space or supplies to offer.

After an hour of harried work, Guillermo, with his frizzed salt-and-pepper hair all but standing on end, gathered the adults for a more complete briefing. Alicia noticed that Lucas wasn't among the crowd, but she still kept searching for him, just in case he'd stayed after she'd brushed him off back by Gabriel's room.

He was nowhere to be found.

Her adrenalized body felt the sharp disappointment of his absence, even if her brain was rushing in a hundred other directions. Right after rejecting him, she hadn't been able to shake his reaction: a barely perceptible slump of his shoulders, the forced smile. While she doubted many people would've been able to detect any of that, she could.

And it made her just as sad as he'd seemed.

As a flock of teens began to shuttle juice boxes out of the kitchen and into the main area for the newcomers, Alicia fidgeted. She wished Lucas were here; he would be able to help during this emergency perhaps more than anyone else.

Where was he? Didn't he know that now, more than ever, Refugio Salvo needed him?

That maybe other people might need him, too?

"We are not sure of the numbers yet," Guillermo was saying in Spanish, "but we could be taking in at least twenty boys. The girls from the fire will be directed elsewhere since this is not a coed facility."

"Where will they be sheltered?" Alicia asked.

"Our Lady of the Lost Souls, for the time being.

This means the nuns will be busy minding the girls at the convent, as well as relocating them."

Another volunteer from Rosarito Beach, a wealthy housewife named Sylvia, asked, "How will we handle this overflow without supplies and manpower?"

"There are food and medical items en route as we speak. Also, arrangements are being made for us to receive temporary mobile homes until new buildings can be constructed. We also have more volunteers on the way from the U.S."

They all just stood there gaping at Guillermo's mustache for a moment. How… What…

But then Alicia knew. She just did.

Lucas.

She bit her lip to hold back the gratefulness and adoration she felt for him as, somehow, she took in Guillermo's instructions for what each volunteer would be doing when the newcomers arrived.

Her heart seemed to grow to twice its size, swelling with a warmth she could barely contain. She waited until her boss dismissed everyone before asking to speak with him alone.

The older man impatiently smoothed down his wiry hair.

"This won't take long, sir," she said. "But I'd just like to… Is Lucas Chandler behind all of this?"

"The benefactor wishes to remain anonymous, Alicia."

She recalled the flashes of all those cameras around Lucas, the reporters following at his heels a few days ago. Why would he keep his kindness a secret now? Unless…

Her stomach felt hollow. Unless she was wrong and someone else was actually behind the donations.

But she wanted to think of Lucas as a hero because, in spite of all the gossip, that's what she saw in him; a man who hadn't been forced to tuck Gabriel into bed or to play checkers with the boys when the cameras weren't around.

Guillermo must've sensed her disquietude. And why not? She was probably wearing it like a wilted corsage.

The administrator patted her arm. "Between you and me, Mr. Chandler will be returning soon. As soon as I told him about the fire, he summoned his helicopter to take him to the damaged site so he could offer help. I hear the vehicle was also being used to evacuate the wounded to the nearest hospital on an unofficial basis."

Yes, a hero. There could never have been a doubt.

"Thank you," she said to her boss, already on her way out of the kitchen, powered by a pattering pulse, inspired by the validation of her faith in a man who couldn't seem to believe in himself half as much as she did.

Heart pumping, she helped set out food and supplies in the common area, items that had already been donated from nearby businesses. Then she aided in putting together the makeshift beds that the older boys had volunteered to sleep in until the newcomers could get their own quarters. As they all worked together, Alicia hugged and encouraged everyone, taking strength from the common bond of helping those in need.

It was almost enough to make her forget about how

Lucas was affecting her, how she couldn't forget who he was and, more importantly, who *she* was.

But when a cry of "He's here!" went up from the boys, she was jerked out of her determination to remain cool and removed.

As she hurried to where the children were gathered by the front windows, she heard Guillermo trying to organize everyone. From outside she could hear a faint chopping whir, and her chest seemed to expand with the throbbing of her heart.

The taller boys made room for her, resting their hands on her shoulders as they craned for a view.

"There's Señor Chandler," said Roberto the painter, pointing out the window to a helicopter that was landing in the near distance. It hovered over a hill, blades spinning, then landed.

Then carrying a blanket-wrapped child in his arms, Lucas emerged from over the hill, his light brown hair waving in the wind, his fine shirt and pants clinging to the muscles of his athletic body.

The moment seemed chipped in time to her, a mental snapshot that made her bones turn to liquid.

Six boys wearing tattered clothing and dark facial smudges followed Lucas as he led them toward the orphanage. While he approached, Alicia saw that he was holding a toddler, his thick arms wrapped around the child, one hand cradling the boy's head to his shoulder.

In that moment, she truly gave him her heart.

"Welcome our new brothers!" she heard Guillermo shout.

The boys at the window excitedly broke apart, but Alicia couldn't move.

She was still caught up in watching Lucas, the man who claimed he was nothing more than a walking bad reputation.

As he came closer, he glanced at the window, saw her standing there, then slowed his steps.

It looked as if he was seeing every one of her confused needs and emotions laid out bare on her face. And it looked as if maybe, just maybe, he felt the same way.

Time disappeared as if it didn't even exist, stopping her heartbeat, stopping all motion around her.

How she wished she could be held against him, too. She wanted to go to him, to tell him that all she really did want was to be with him, even if the mere thought was ridiculous.

The boys flung open the door, allowing in the sound of the chopper as it took off again, allowing in the first wide-eyed newcomers.

As the room spun into action, she remembered what was important right now—securing the newcomers. She tore her gaze away from Lucas and rushed to greet the boys. Fighting her trembling limbs, she bent to their height, welcoming them with smiles and reassurance— her specialties.

But the good-hearted older Refugio Salvo orphans wanted to welcome the new boys, too, and they ended up leading them away for snacks and drinks as two staff doctors waited nearby to begin checking the arrivals over.

The back of Alicia's neck tingled.

She looked over her shoulder to find Lucas standing there, the child clinging to him as if he never wanted to let go.

The man's eyes were dark, fraught with the twilight colors of something Alicia couldn't explain as he consumed her with his gaze. Overcome, she stood, facing him, caught in his magnetism, her body quivering.

"You took care of everything," she said, voice ragged with the happiness and terror of seeing him.

Lucas moved toward her, his presence swallowing her.

"I'll always take care of everything," he said. "Always."

The words were still ringing in Lucas's ears as Alicia's eyes widened.

When he'd heard about the fire, he hadn't thought to do anything but call his pilot to warm up the chopper, fly down the coast to the site of the destruction, then offer any help he could. On the way to his transportation, he'd also called David to see if he could work their connections to procure more volunteers and supplies. Then he'd gotten a hold of Guillermo Ramos to provide whatever he needed for Refugio Salvo, whether it was money, food, buildings or all of the above.

When David had mentioned getting some reporters over to the orphanage to cover this "jackpot," Lucas had denied him. This wasn't about PR—in fact, it hadn't even entered his mind until his brother had brought it up.

"And, if I see any cameras around," Lucas had said, "I *will* eat them for dinner."

David knew when his sibling was serious, so he hadn't called the press. At least, not as far as Lucas knew.

Obviously he hadn't analyzed his intentions, at first, but on the chopper ride back, as he'd taken care of the traumatized children, he'd realized just why it was so important to help in secret. He needed to do the right thing and to do it because he *wanted* to, just as Alicia would have.

Maybe, that way, he'd actually deserve this woman who stood in front of him now with her heart in her eyes.

He was so mired in what this tragedy had brought on that being direct with her seemed the only way to communicate. Back at the other orphanage, he'd seen the smoldering foundation of what had once been a home. He'd seen some of the orphans who'd lived there choppered to the hospital with third-degree burns, had seen the staff weeping because they were so grateful that no one had died.

"Life is short and sweet," an old man with burns covering his hands and face had said to Lucas as he'd helped him onto the first chopper out. He'd tried to smile even around his charred skin. "I'm so lucky to still be alive."

Still alive, Lucas thought, hugging the orphan. *So make the most of life while you have it.*

As he and Alicia faced each other, the room bustled around them: orphans getting to know each other, little boys crying from the horror of the fire as others attempted to console them. Lucas had even called in counselors who would arrive tonight, because he meant what he'd said to Alicia.

He could take care of everything. And he would.

Guillermo Ramos came over to take the new orphan from Lucas. As the boy was lifted away, Lucas held out a hand as if it felt too empty without anything to fill it anymore.

But then, as if Alicia knew just what he needed, she enfolded his fingers in hers.

The contact was so profound that Lucas almost lost it. He'd never craved a touch so much—her touch.

He held her hand against his heart. At the contact, it pumped double-time.

As if shocked, Alicia froze, her gaze confused.

Right, Lucas thought. *She told me she can't be alone with me. I remember now.*

Firmly back in reality, the rest of the room came into focus. Gabriel, with his tousled hair, darted out of the hallway and across the floor, from group to group, handing out juice boxes. Lucas's pulse jumped at the sight of the child, an orphan who could've just as easily been caught in that fire and hurt—or even worse—today.

Shockingly, he realized he couldn't stand the thought of not having the boy around. Lucas felt so much more like an actual human being when Gabe was smiling at him, shooting him that gaze that said he thought Lucas was pretty decent.

Alicia noticed the little host, too.

Still touching her hand—could she feel the vibration of his pulse through it?—he squeezed it, connecting with her over their fondness for the boy.

"Gabriel's in his element, isn't he?" she said.

Her voice was rough, as if she were forcing it out of her.

"Alicia…"

Maybe it was the way he'd said her name, because she interrupted.

"I know I'm not supposed to be aware of what you've done today, but…thank you so much. You—" She shook her head. "You've gone above and beyond. Why don't you want anyone to know about it?"

It sounded as if his simple activities had made her admire him even more. He glowed with the confidence she had in him.

"It's nothing anybody else wouldn't do," he said.

"Oh, no," she said, head tilting as she seemed to look into him with a gaze that was just this side of reverent. "Don't tell me you're not buying into your own heroics?"

Looking at her, he could *almost* believe he was that savior.

Not knowing how to react, Lucas watched as Gabe gaily approached one of the lightly burned children who was waiting for medical attention. Then, with the open curiosity only the young could get away with, he inspected the boy's wounds. The disturbing sight of Gabe's smooth, unblemished skin against the other boy's injuries made Lucas fist his hands until his nails dug into his palms.

"Life can be so short," he said softly, realizing what was really important now. Realizing he had it right in his hands.

She'd also turned to glance at Gabe and the other child, but now, biting her lower lip, she turned back to him. He knew she understood just what he'd seen down at the fire site.

She slowly raised her other hand toward him, hesitated. Then something flared in her eyes, golden and open, and she reached the rest of the way toward his face, cupping his jaw.

He shivered at the power of her touch.

She paused, seeming to trip on her words, but then finally released them. "I missed you."

Jarred with surprise, Lucas leaned his cheek into her palm.

In a flash of all-consuming light, he knew what he wanted. His mind swam, blocking common sense, barring anything but a deep need his instincts knew how to feed now, only with the threat of tragedy hovering over his head.

He saw his future in front of him: a gentle, loving woman who believed in him the way Alicia did, a family—a son?—to complete what didn't necessarily have to be an illusion…

Do it, his impulse urged. *With people who believe in you, you can do* anything.

He looked into Alicia's eyes, drowning in them. On this surge of adrenaline and fear, his crazy emotions seemed like tiny epiphanies merging into an inevitable burst of reason.

He'd wanted her from the first second he'd seen her. He'd seen lives explode today. So why wait to grab what he already knew he needed?

"How much?" His words sounded distant, as if spoken by a better man. "How much did you miss me, Alicia?"

She bit her lip, closed her eyes.

He spoke his heart before his brain could catch up. "I want you to come home with me. I want you to—" holy crap, he was really saying it "—always be with me."

At first, the words didn't register. *Always be with me?*

They swirled, mixing with all the scenarios she'd created about home, hearth, Lucas and Gabriel.

What was he saying?

I'm wondering, Lucas had told her earlier today, *how long it actually takes to realize it's the right time with someone.*

Her temples were beating in time to her pulse. "I'm not... I don't..."

He seemed feverish as he led her into the hallway, where they had more privacy. During the short trip there, Alicia stumbled, halfway breathless with disbelief. What was happening?

When they got to a quiet spot, he turned her to face him, hands on her shoulders. His touch seemed to burn through her blouse.

"Alicia, I know how I feel about you. Time's not going to convince me of any more."

And how's that? she wanted to ask just to be sure. But her tongue was still tied.

He rushed on. "I'm going back to the States, but

something happened down here…things, day by day, that have made me realize what I'm missing in my life. And now, seeing how it could all disappear in a bunch of flames…I want you to be with me. Especially since—"

He cupped her face with his hands, his touch warm, the embodiment of all her nighttime dreams.

"Since I want Gabe to be around, too," he said.

Several things hit her: Joy that her favorite orphan— one everybody thought was unadoptable—had found a father. Happiness that Lucas had discovered something he was missing.

And that something was her. Right? Because she still couldn't believe what he was saying. How? Why?

Lucas bent closer in the dim light, eyes wide and wild, as if he were having a fervid dream. "I want us to be a family, Alicia. I want you to *marry* me."

It was as if a fist had reached into her and jerked, stripping out the wires that held her together, making her spark with excitement and fear.

"We barely…" She stopped because she didn't have enough oxygen to continue.

"I realize that. But I also know that you and Gabe belong in my life."

She thought of how she'd nearly imploded after he'd appeared from behind the hill, thought of how she just might feel that way every time he stepped through the door of their home.

A home, she thought, trembling.

"This is all moving so fast," she said, "I can't think—"

"Don't think," he said. "*Feel.* And I know you do feel something for me, Alicia."

Heat engulfed her. He knew. She hadn't been able to hide her affection at all. So why was she still fighting it?

Something unfettered by rules, something instinctive, wondered why she couldn't just take a chance, as she'd done when she moved down here from San Diego. She'd been born with that impulsiveness, even if she'd squashed it under a need to control her life. And he was offering her everything she wanted, so why not seize the day?

Use common sense, she thought. *Your parents dived in, and look what happened.*

And she wasn't them. Not if she could help it.

"Happiness has its price," she said, touching her charm bracelet, her souvenir from a father who'd been impetuous, too.

"And they call me the cynical one?" He laughed, stroking her hair back now. His voice was low, rough with emotion. "Happiness is having a real family you can depend on. Happiness is having enough money at your disposal to give to any charity that you want."

The picnic under the oak tree rushed back to her. He'd asked what she would do for the opportunity to have an endless amount of money for good works, for more redemption.

Had he been thinking of marrying her then? Had this been love at first sight for him, just as…

She flinched. Just as it had been for her, too?

It was true. Undeniably, shockingly true.

"Don't say no," he said, stroking his thumbs over her cheeks. "I can't—I *won't* leave without you. I can't imagine going back and never seeing you again or leaving you here while we trade e-mails or phone calls or… Alicia, just come with me."

She wouldn't choose to go a day without him or Gabriel, either. But… "I won't live in sin with you, Lucas."

He stiffened. "I would never ask you to do that. I know this is so fast, but leaving you and Gabe behind is out of the question. I'd rather marry you down here and take you back home as my wife. Come with me. You know this is right for all of us."

Her mind was whirling, her chest heavy with the weight of what he was laying on her.

She didn't even argue about the option of him staying in Mexico. When it came right down to it, this wasn't her real home, so she would never ask it of him. She wanted to settle in a place full of love, and that would be wherever Gabriel and this man were. Location wasn't the issue. Besides, staying down here while Gabriel was with Lucas…

She couldn't imagine it.

He must've taken her hesitation as a lead-up to rejection, because his shoulders seemed to slump a little. But then he seemed to stiffen, as if taking a big breath and jumping in.

"You make me a better man," he said quietly, voice racked with emotion so naked that she couldn't fully absorb it. "Can't you see that?"

In the dim hallway, she could barely discern his features. But she didn't have to. His tone told her everything: that he didn't believe in himself, that maybe she was the only one who'd ever given him the chance to make something more out of a tarnished reputation. It broke her heart.

"I swear to you," he said, "No more playboy or dare-devil. Just a good husband and his angel."

Angel.

She slipped her hands up his arms, wanting so badly to comfort him, wanting so badly to be that angel. His muscles clenched under her palms, and she recalled how these arms had held that orphan as he'd come out of the helicopter, how he could hold her and Gabriel like that, too.

There were so many reasons to say yes.

But one thought kept echoing through her: respect. Marriage could erase the sins of her father and prove that she, his daughter, could live a decent personal life. It would show him, wherever he was, that she was nothing like him at all.

So tempting—the answer she'd been looking for. The solution to everything.

"Miss Alicia?" called a little voice. As it echoed down the hallway, she saw the shadow of a boy appear. "Miss Alicia!"

Gabriel, the son of her heart. The boy she could provide for if she only said yes.

He began running toward her. Toward *them*.

The people who could be his family.

In spite of her doubts about this going too fast, in spite of the shock she knew her spiritual advisors would display, an answer to Lucas's proposal rushed out of her, riding on pure emotion.

"Yes," she said. "Yes, I'll marry you."

Dios. Too risky, too—

He took her hands and, with an ecstatic laugh, pulled her to him. His chest was wide and firm, his arms like a haven that would keep trouble away.

Gabriel crashed into both of them.

As it was always meant to be, Lucas swooped the child into their embrace, and Alicia felt the borders of her heart fully connect, as if completed.

But panicked common sense screamed at her to take it back, to be real about this….

"Guess what, Gabe?" Lucas said, pointing to him and then her. "You're going to have a mommy and daddy!"

His meaning must've been obvious to the love-starved child, because he hopped up and down, squealing and hugging both of them.

As Lucas drew her into a hug with him and Gabriel, she thought that, yes, sure, certainly this *was* the best choice she could ever make.

Even if she still couldn't believe she'd made it.

Chapter Seven

Two days later, Lucas lingered just outside the main building of Refugio Salvo where the orphans had first welcomed him with refreshments and shy smiles.

But today, under a clouded screen of sunshine, there were canapés instead of burritos and petits fours instead of cookies. There was a piñata hanging from a nearby tree, amusing a crowd of children, including the ringleader, Gabe. There was a mariachi band in traditional dress, singing in full-throated abandon while strumming their guitars. Guests wore flowered dresses and suits while sipping champagne and posing for pictures for carefully selected photographers.

His wedding reception.

He'd actually said the vows, Lucas thought, still a

little shell-shocked. Now that the flood of emotion from the fire had worn off, he was able to think clearly about what he'd done: married Alicia. The big *M*.

Funny thing was, he'd believed every word he'd been persuading her with at the time—he'd felt that she really was his salvation and he'd warmed to the spontaneous notion of having Gabriel with them. He had a soft spot for the child and he could do so much for him—much more than even an orphanage.

But then reality had hit. He'd realized that, for Alicia, this was true affection. He knew it from the cloud-nine smile she'd been wearing for the past couple of days, ever since he'd proposed so dramatically. So many times, Lucas had wanted to correct what he'd done, to be a big man about this and make up for the heat of a whirlwind moment....

But then David had heard the news and congratulated him. He'd even looked at Lucas with something like awe, marveling that he'd taken the relationship suggestion and gone "the extra mile" for TCO with a wife and a child, to boot. Lucas hadn't explained that everything had come from a moment of madness. No—he'd *liked* the admiration from his normally superior brother, even as he'd felt dirty and dishonest. And, when his father had called to congratulate him in a tone that didn't include derision or impatience? Game over.

Now, more than ever, Lucas knew Alicia would help him wash the dirt off. Their marriage really could be the cure-all for his misspent life.

In the aftermath, Lucas and David had pulled many a string to cover the details as soon as possible, since the Brain believed practical Alicia might come to her senses and cancel the whole thing soon. While Lucas had bristled at that because it was niggling at him, too, he also knew Alicia would never go back on her word. Not after they'd promised Gabe in the heat of the moment that he was going to have a family.

The last thing Alicia would ever do, was break her favorite orphan's heart. Lucas would swear to that.

But, he thought, there was something else that was keeping her true to the proposal.

All I want is a family, she'd told him during their oak-tree picnic. And then there was the way she watched him, the way she'd kissed him.

God, what had he done?

They'd been so damned busy with this whirlwind event, as well as getting the new orphans settled, that they'd barely spent time together. Not the way they used to, anyway, with privacy, intimacy, even that shy kiss. Lucas missed it and he even found himself wondering when he'd feel her lips against his again, when he'd get to be a true husband to her.

But…one thing at a time. He was determined to leave the physical decisions to Alicia. His conscience wouldn't allow any other option, even if his sex drive was raging at him.

While she'd spent the past couple of days putting together her wedding finery, David had brought an army of TCO assistants to arrange everything from the flowers decorating the area, to the cake, to securing a couple of handpicked reporters to cover the event. One assistant had even flown in the Chandler family's regular preacher for these last-minute out-door nuptials.

"We'll have an even bigger wedding any way you want it after we get settled in New York," he'd promised Alicia. "A church, the works. I just want you to be with me and Gabe as soon as possible, that's all." And he'd meant it.

She'd agreed to the rushed ceremony, not wanting to "live in sin," as she'd told him before. But he detected hesitation, nonetheless.

He knew that her nun friends had been emphatically arguing for her not to go through with this so soon, but she seemed to be forging on against their advice. Maybe it was because every time he saw her, he stressed the urgency of their union, how quickly he wanted them to become a family and make Gabe happy. He'd even enlisted TCO's best attorneys to facilitate the marriage and fast-track the adoption, utilizing every powerful, politically connected Chandler family resource to allow Lucas and Alicia to bring their new son home to the States.

And his hard-sell marriage idea—his ticket to respect—was working, even if reluctance did pass over her features before he kissed her forehead in a chaste farewell and blasted off to make more arrangements.

Lucas's searching gaze found her as she emerged from the building, surrounded by other female orphanage volunteers. Even though they were all celebrating with his new wife, Lucas could tell they were worried about this quickie marriage, too. Every look they shot him said, *You'd better take good care of her.*

But he would. In fact, all he wanted to do was make her happy.

As she walked down the stairs, a headpiece sans veil collecting her upswept curls, he couldn't take his eyes off her. His chest ached at the sight of his bride holding a bouquet of white flowers and wearing a simple, roomy, long white dress. It had scalloped sleeves and embroidery, lending the outfit an old-fashioned dignity. Her ample curves filled it out, and his belly heated with pure...lust.

Yup, lust. That had to be all there was to it. He didn't love her. He couldn't. And, somehow, he'd gotten around ever having to say it to her.

Was that because she just assumed how he must feel? How? He couldn't have shown her any evidence of it because it didn't exist in him. Chandler men didn't know how to love.

Images and feelings from the night of the fire came barging back: The sublime joy at seeing her again; the loving look on her face as she'd been watching his approach through the window; the crazy thought that life is short and she would make his own existence so much better....

Alicia had stopped halfway down the stairs, the other women continuing to walk past her until they filtered into the rest of the crowd.

"Listen, listen!" yelled Guillermo Ramos as he climbed up the steps to stand next to Alicia.

He'd assumed the responsibilities of host, even though Lucas suspected the man wasn't fully convinced this wedding was the best choice for his diligent worker, either. But, like Lucas, the man clearly wanted her to be happy, so he was throwing himself into helping.

Alicia seemed to have that effect on everyone.

Guillermo had the crowd's attention, except for the boys smacking the piñata with a stick in the background. He'd spoken in English for the sake of the groom's U.S. guests.

Truthfully, Lucas didn't know most of them because David had invited family friends he'd flown out on one of their jets for appearances' sake. Lucas's "friends"— party buddies, mainly—hadn't been invited.

Sad thing was, Lucas didn't really miss them much.

"Thank you again for attending this celebration at Refugio Salvo," Guillermo added.

Amidst the applause, the administrator swept his hand around to indicate the grounds, and Lucas smiled to himself, knowing how proud Guillermo was of his hard work.

"We have experienced hard times here," he continued, "but they have been met with determination and great love from our staff and our patron, Lucas Chandler."

Here, Guillermo turned to Lucas, raising his glass of punch in salute.

In his corner, Lucas merely nodded, needled by the secrets he was keeping from his bride, the woman who was also raising her glass to him, her face flushed, her eyes full of adoration.

It was as if she were inside Lucas, nestling into a place that had always been meant for her.

He broke eye contact, knowing he didn't deserve the affection. He didn't deserve her, period.

"Join me," Guillermo added, turning his attention back to the guests, "in recognizing our patron and our beautiful Alicia, who has volunteered so much of her time to us and, she has reassured me, will continue to do so from afar."

"Hear! Hear!" someone in the crowd said as they all toasted, then drank. Soon afterward, one of the female orphanage volunteers started lobbying for Alicia to throw her bouquet. Lucas wondered how he was going to get through this.

He pictured the end of the party, when he could finally relax as the sun set. He'd fall into bed, close his eyes and…

An unexpected element entered that picture: Alicia snuggling against him, Gabe burrowing against his other side.

The thought should've panicked him, but he actually felt calmer. He held the picture in his head, allowing it to lead him to the end of the day.

"Woolgathering?" said a soft voice beside him.

Lucas shook off the fantasy, finding Sister Elisabeth standing there. Always freshly scrubbed, her skin smooth, her cheeks rounded, she was one of only two nuns who'd attended.

She'd requested to talk with him for the past couple of days and he'd deftly managed to avoid any chats. So he was thrown off balance by her approach.

A cheer went up as Alicia threw her bouquet. The flowers bounced off a guest's head and into another nun's arms. Sister Maria-Rosa, the strict one. She seemed stunned to be holding the bouquet as the crowd laughed and applauded.

"I've got a lot to think about," he said to Sister Elisabeth, making an attempt at joviality.

"I suppose you do and I'm here to show support for that very notion." The nun glanced over at the piñata, where Gabe was hopping up and down, waiting for his turn to take a whack at the colorful mock donkey. "You're taking on quite a bit, Mr. Chandler. Both you *and* Alicia."

He watched Gabe, too, thankful that the boy was in a good mood today. "I'll hire a top-notch child psychologist to help him along and to give us advice on parenting."

"Gabriel will need more than that. Are you ready to sacrifice all the time you enjoyed as a bachelor?"

Sacrifice. Even though Lucas had no delusions about how much effort Gabe would take, he'd never thought of the investment as a sacrifice. It was easy to admit that he dug the boy, faults and all. Every kid needed someone to feel that way about them or else…

Lucas thought of himself, of all the nannies who'd raised him and David, of all the social events he'd been forced to go to where he'd been a miniature man in a tiny suit who was expected to be seen and not heard. And, when he hadn't obeyed, there'd been hell to pay.

He wouldn't let that happen to Gabe. He'd never try to kill the love of life in him, just help to make it manageable—just as he was learning, himself, right?

The sound of silverware against glass caught Lucas's attention, and he glanced over to David, who'd emerged from skulking about the fringes and was calling for a kiss between the bride and groom. Lucas's hackles went up because he knew his brother wasn't just drunk and celebrating.

He'd taken over, reminding Lucas of what today was really about. Reminding Lucas, as well, that their father had supposedly been too ill to make it to the wedding….

"Kiss! Kiss!" yelled the guests.

Sister Elisabeth touched his arm. "God be with you. Even if this is abrupt, I've got a lot of faith in you."

Although her honesty nagged him, he nodded, glancing at the steps, at Alicia, who was blushing amidst the clamor.

Blushing. He'd never known someone to do it so much. It touched a nerve, made him feel protective of a woman who still had such innocence.

Too bad he was the biggest threat to that.

He came to stand a step below his bride, bringing them almost face-to-face. Her lips were so red, so desirable. Her perfume slid its way into his pores, his every sense, invading him with the warmth of musky flowers.

He realized that, with all the pomp and circumstance, they hadn't been this close since their chaste wedding kiss.

"Hi," she said.

"Hi." The word seemed to scrape his throat.

This near, guilt was flaying him bare, revealing the tender streak that had felt so natural the other night, when he'd proposed.

"Kiss, kiss…"

"Guess we've got to quiet them down," he said softly.

She pressed her lips together, her gaze on his own mouth. It was as if she was already tasting him.

"Kiss, kiss…"

Even though he moved toward her slowly, the staccato of his heartbeat made time rush. Just before he made contact, he heard her inhale, and his veins seized up, stopping his pulse.

As he pressed his lips to hers, he went deaf. Nothing existed but being with her, the kiss enclosing them in something like a snow globe, a fantasy world where nothing else could get in. Heaviness flowed through him, over him, washing him clean and infusing him with passion.

Without thinking, he slid his hand behind her head, then down to the graceful slant of her neck. He felt the bump of her nape, the softness of her skin.

In the comforting darkness of his desire for her, he saw a flash. Felt it rip through him. Then another. And another.

Cameras, he thought hazily. *We're not alone.*

Reluctantly, he broke away, his opened eyes greeted by those flashes. His hearing came back, ushering in loud cheers.

He pretended to recover by slipping an arm around Alicia's shoulders and waving to the crowd, even though he was shaken to the core.

A kiss, he thought. One damn kiss.

"Smile, angel," he heard himself saying. "Just keep smiling."

She stiffened, and he sympathized, holding her closer in the glare of the camera flashes.

Protecting her from himself.

* * *

At the airstrip, dust blew through the air as Alicia entered the tiny terminal, where she headed for the restroom. She'd told Lucas and Gabriel that she needed to freshen up before the reporters arrived to take pictures of their departure, but that had been a lie.

Angel, she thought again, the word running through her like an alarm that had been set to go off every hour since the reception. *He keeps calling me angel.*

She busted into the bathroom and rested her clutch purse on the metal shelf under the mirror. Bracing her hands on the sink, she peered into the looking glass, wondering just who was reflected back at her.

A crazy woman she barely knew, curls still held at bay by a pearl barrette, cheeks colored with two spots of red, body encased in a formfitting off-white two-piece suit that one of the TCO stylists had purchased for her.

The *new* her?

Alicia turned on the water and splashed her face. No, she was still the *old* her, the one who'd made this wild decision that was scrambling her life. The girl who'd spent the last couple of days busying herself with wedding preparations because she'd been racked with guilt about telling Lucas who he was really marrying.

No angel. That was for sure.

Water dripped from her face and into the sink. Every sound was a poke to her conscience. What would Lucas do if he knew she was tainted? He wouldn't love her, that's what would happen. He could have any woman in the world, yet he'd chosen her because she made him a better man.

She almost laughed at that. If only he knew. She doubted it would take him two days to realize he belonged with one of his own set.

But she was going to make it up to him in spades because no one could take away the family she'd finally found. She'd be the perfect wife and live up to every expectation he had for her. Deep down, she believed he wanted the same thing—love. True love.

Yes, she'd definitely made the right choice. Definitely. Especially where Gabriel was concerned.

At the thought of the boy they were adopting, Alicia perked up, thinking that the end justified the means. As soon as Lucas's money rushed the adoption papers through, Gabriel would get his stable home and so much more. She would give him all the love in the world while doing the same for Lucas, another person whom she suspected needed someone to just understand him.

Renewed for the time being, she dried her face, grabbed her purse, then strode out of the restroom, determined to confront her new responsibilities.

But when she heard a voice echoing through the small, quiet lobby, she paused. Lucas?

With a burst of beatitude, she went toward the sound, turning the corner with a smile so wide it almost hurt.

Her heart fell when she saw it was only David, his back to her, a cell raised to his head and a finger plugging his other ear. She wasn't sure what to think of Lucas's hard-as-nails brother, yet, and now wasn't the time for her to sort it out.

Before she could leave, she caught a piece of his conversation.

"Oh, yeah, she's our secret weapon with the demographic here. She's gold."

Demographic? What was he talking about—an employee with TCO?

Feeling like a little girl who'd walked in on an adult discussion, Alicia took a couple of steps away, backtracking around the corner. But when David started turning around while unplugging his other ear, she automatically pretended she was just rounding the wall.

"Oh…" she said, feigning surprise.

Cool as silk, David nodded to her. "Uh-huh, uh-huh," he said to the person on the other end of the line.

She held up a hand in acknowledgment of him, then pointed to the tarmac, where the family jet was waiting. The other, larger one, which had transported some wedding guests, would depart tomorrow morning.

Without sticking around for David's response, she headed for the exit.

TCO business. David had been talking about one of his female employees, that's all. The corporation had interests all over the world, including Mexico…

At least, that's what she kept telling herself.

She spotted Lucas by the stairs that led up to the jet's entrance and her brain futzed, like a television station that had closed down for the night.

He was bending to Gabriel, brushing some dust or grime or whatever the heck the child had gotten into off his leg. But Lucas wasn't chiding him as one of the nuns would have. He was smiling, as if he enjoyed the chore. As if understanding that children got dirty and that was okay.

She approached them. "Damage control?"

When he looked up, her pulse jammed, veins tangling.

"Gabe here decided to pretend he was an ant crawling on the ground with food on his back." Lucas stood, tweaking the boy's cheek as Gabriel glowed up at him. "I already tried to get the grit out of his pants."

With one look, she saw that Lucas hadn't been too successful.

"Gabriel, you're so funny," she said, joking with him in a pattern they'd established long ago.

"*You're* funny, Miss Alicia."

All of them laughed and, for the first time in hours, she felt good. They'd returned to how everything had been before the chaos of the last few days. It was almost as if they were playing Wiffle ball again or as if they were laying Gabriel down for a nap.

A warm glow settled in her, nesting.

"Ready to go to your new home?" Lucas asked the boy, hefting him up into his arms.

Gabriel's mouth pursed as he went, "Hmm." Alicia knew that meant he was confused and he didn't know how to express himself, so she translated into both Spanish and child speak.

The boy lit up. "Yes. Ready."

"Yes, *Papa*," Alicia said, without thinking. Then the weight of reality settled on her. "You can call him Papa now."

Lucas seemed to realize what was going on at the same time. He looked winded, stunned. But then he burst into that stellar grin, holding Gabriel to his chest.

"That's right," he said, voice hoarse with emotion. "I'm your papa."

As Gabriel threw his arms around Lucas's neck, tears began to sting Alicia's eyes.

"And husband," Lucas whispered.

She sobbed once, then went to her new family, holding them against her. Somewhere in the distance, she heard a car drive up, but nothing else mattered right now, and she had no idea how long it was until she heard the slam of doors. Closer, David's voice sounded behind them.

"Showtime," said Lucas's brother. "The big love story that's going to plaster tomorrow's papers. 'Lucas Chandler's whirlwind marriage.' Every woman in the world is going to swoon."

The echo of David's demographic conversation haunted the back of her mind, but she was too busy feeling robbed to care much. Of course they were going to use this wedding as publicity; what concerned her more was the fact that, at David's interruption, her family had separated from one another.

Alicia wanted to ask why pictures were necessary when they already had so many from the wedding. Then she remembered who she was now.

Lucas Chandler's wife.

So she got ready to pose, trying to persuade herself that she really belonged in the same frame with this man.

That he hadn't made a mistake, at all.

* * *

They'd been in the air for two hours when Gabe finally succumbed to the pressure of his new situation.

The boy had been playing with a puzzle at a table. It was one among many amusements Lucas had ordered for the flight, knowing that Gabe's normally scheduled nap would take up only so much time and the child might want to expend some creative energy. David was in a private room at the rear of the plane, knee-deep in business, of course.

As for Alicia, he'd made sure she was comfortably settled on a sofa with a pillow and blanket. She'd hinted at needing her own nap after the excitement of takeoff had subsided and, as a new husband, he probably should've joined her, holding her hand, cuddling with her. But he was too on edge to even be in the same area, too racked with the reality of what he'd done.

To make matters worse, he'd caught the questions in her gaze as he'd left to be with Gabe.

Why aren't you spending time with me?

Little did she know that this was only the beginning. Now that the press had been given their big romance story and the official marriage documents had been signed, he could move on to his other plans to save TCO.

Reluctant to glance back at her—to *go* back to her—Lucas headed for his new son. It was so much easier to be close to Gabe than Alicia. So much simpler to admit that he was allowed to have affection for the boy.

Who the hell knew why?

At the sight of Gabe sticking his tongue out of his mouth as he concentrated on the puzzle, Lucas breathed a sigh of relief. Gabe wouldn't demand anything from him.

But, fifteen minutes later, when the boy used his arm to wipe the pieces off the table in a fit of sudden anger, Lucas rethought his assessment of the situation.

Gabe fisted his hands over the mess, spouting a gush of Spanish words that couldn't have been pretty.

"What is it?" Lucas tried a Spanish phrase Alicia had taught him; he'd already tried to learn some in order to communicate better with the boy. *"Que pasa?"*

Another tangle of Spanish words came out of the kid's mouth, and somewhere in there, Lucas thought he heard him say, "Too hard!"

"Then, you can play something else," Lucas said, thinking he had this all locked up.

But the exhaustion of the day, coupled with all these changes, must've been doing a number on Gabe. He gave a loud cry, then smacked the table.

"Hey, now." Lucas held on to the boy's hands so he wouldn't hurt himself.

The boy was having none of it. He pulled away, eyes getting red and teary as he shook his head, sobbed and jerked away from Lucas.

Okay, he wasn't sure how to handle this, after all. Was it cool to try to hug him? Yeah, right, as if that was going to make everything all better. Should he let Gabe cry himself out? He couldn't imagine just sitting here while the boy carried on.

But he was going to be his *father* now. Shouldn't he know what to do, even instinctively?

What have you gotten yourself into?

Thankfully Alicia had come over and taken a seat next to Gabe. Her bracelet rattled as she reached out to the boy.

"Gabriel." Then she said something in Spanish.

Anxious, Lucas leaned on the table, wanting to help, but feeling that he had nothing to contribute.

But then she glanced up at him, gaze soft, drawing him back into the inner circle linked together by man, woman and child.

Home, he thought. *She's more home than I've ever had.*

Why did that scare him so much?

"Your new papa is here, too," she said, clearly translating for Lucas while repeating the words in Spanish for Gabe. "And your papa's not going anywhere, either. He's bringing us to a new home. We're a family now and we won't ever leave you. Do you understand that?"

Gabe's breath stuttered as he sucked it in, his eyes wide and dark, hopeful.

But as much as Alicia's words were comforting the boy, they were bothering Lucas. He found that he wanted so badly to believe in them, wanted to know that Alicia wouldn't leave if she found out what he'd done to her and Gabe, wanted to always be assured that someone in his life stayed, unlike his mother or his serial-husband father or his move-on-to-the-next-adventure friends.

Gabe reached up his arms for Alicia, snuggling into her embrace, and she rocked him while singing a sweet tune.

Note by note, Lucas allowed the song to get to him, too, even if he thought it might be best to keep it out.

Chapter Eight

The first thing Alicia and Lucas did upon arriving at their penthouse was to tuck a completely exhausted Gabriel into bed. The mattress was the biggest she'd ever seen, the guest room already custom outfitted with pictures of *Sesame Street* characters and toys. She was stunned by the efficiency of Lucas's assistants, as well as the decadence of the penthouse…or, rather, her new home.

Yes, she kept telling herself, home, where she belonged.

Afterward, even as Alicia was still reeling from the shock that she, *she* was going to live in this luxurious place, the head of the household, Ms. Boland, gave her a tour. Lucas excused himself to make a phone call while the proper brunette—a young woman who wore a gray business suit, black-rimmed glasses and bunned hair—had gotten her new mistress acclimated. Then, after the personal assistant left, Alicia found herself very alone.

Alienated. Curious. Discombobulated.

Bundled in a new coat that would've been too much for an early winter Mexico night, she wandered onto the terrace, which overlooked Central Park. The cold New York air hit her and she shivered—but not just because of the weather.

I'm really a wife.

Not that Alicia felt like it. During the jet ride, Lucas had almost been a stranger, even if he'd made certain that she was comfortable in every way.

But there'd been something odd about him, as if he were detached. He'd spent most of his time with Gabriel—which she'd loved to watch—or talking in the private back room with David.

It'd seemed as if the only person he hadn't had time for was her—his bride.

Why? Earlier today, during their wedding, he'd kissed Alicia until her legs had just about turned to wet sand. There'd been no lack of passion then, nor a few days ago, when he'd proposed to her so emotionally.

Shouldn't the man who'd talked her into such a headlong move want to cuddle on the plane trip home? Or had he been saving his affection for a time when they could be alone?

She trembled again, her blood tumbling, increasing in temperature. The wedding night. A shared bed.

On a primal level, she was ready for him. But she

was also nervous, fearful of losing control and becoming what she most feared: Her parents. A bad woman who could never wash herself of the past.

She heard a door slide open and shut behind her. Lucas. Every footstep that closed the distance between them thumped inside her chest like cannon shots.

"Beautiful view," he said, voice low. It rode the hairs over her sensitized skin, a verbal stroke, slow and easy.

"The park is much bigger than I ever imagined."

"I'm not talking about the park."

Boom-da-boom went her heart.

He sauntered over, resting his hands on the brick wall while casting her a look brimming with appreciation. She felt like a goddess again, just as she had in her wedding dress, just as she had when he'd proposed to her and she'd believed with every reckless pound of her blood that she'd fallen for him at first sight, and that he'd fallen for her, too.

"You're cold." He shucked off his large tailored wool coat, then slipped it over her own.

The silk lining made his coat slip off her shoulders, the ill fit reminding her that she didn't belong in fine clothing like this at all.

Still, she grabbed at the wool, pulling it around her.

"To the rescue with your coat yet again," she said, referring to their initial meeting, when he'd acted like a gentleman and covered her wet blouse.

"Whatever you need, it's yours." He gestured toward the penthouse. "So what do you think?"

She laughed, indicating that there was no way she couldn't like it. A triplex penthouse at the top of The

Boudin, a historic hotel that attracted the rich and famous. On the limo ride from the airport, Lucas had told her that they would have not only a personal staff but access to a concierge, twenty-four-hour housekeeping, a valet and room service. Its highlights included two terraces, four bedrooms, a library, a media room, a gourmet kitchen, a greenhouse and a small wine cellar. The first floor was an old ballroom, and there were wood-burning fireplaces, crystal chandeliers and marble baths sprinkled amidst the retro-chic furnishings.

He must've translated her pause as polite displeasure. "Maybe it's not to your tastes, huh? I had this decorated when I moved in a few years ago and haven't spent much time here since, with all the traveling I used to do. If you want to redecorate, we'll make arrangements."

His offer pleased her, but she couldn't imagine what in the world she would change about a place like this. "Maybe later. Or…" Absently, she touched the waist-high brick wall, then chanced a peek over it to the long fall below.

A thought shook her. Gabriel. What if he wandered out here?

"Is there a way to childproof the terrace?"

He seemed taken aback, even a little horrified that he hadn't realized this first. "Right. You're right. I'll have it taken care of tomorrow. And we'll get someone to help with Gabe during the day so you can…well, do whatever it is you want to do while I'm at work."

"You're already going back to the office?" They'd agreed to put off a honeymoon until Gabriel knew for certain that this was his real home, but couldn't Lucas at least stick around?

He seemed to catch on to what she was thinking. "Soon we'll take a big trip, okay? You, me and even Gabe."

Her libido didn't love the thought of having to share her husband right now, but every other part of her was content with always keeping Gabriel near. It's what she'd wanted for so long. And, in the end, she would have her husband during the night, anyway, after little boys went off to bed.

She shrugged even farther into the coat. "I wish you could take one day off, Lucas. Just at the beginning…"

His posture straightened. "I really have to go, at least for a few hours. Then…" He paused as if working something out. Seconds later, he offered his killer grin, back to being Mr. Charm. "Then the rest of tomorrow will be yours. I promise. In the meantime, though, there's a stylist who'll be bringing more clothing for your and Gabe's approval in the morning."

He was watching Alicia as if to sift out her reaction to an activity most women loved—shopping. But it'd never been all that enticing to her.

"She'll have some designs for formal wear, too," he added. "You just tell her what you like and it's yours."

"Formal wear?"

"Get ready to be introduced to New York, angel. First up, we're officially meeting my dad at a restaurant the day after tomorrow, when he feels better. He'll meet Gabe this weekend, in a more comfortable setting for the boy, like here at home. Then there's a holiday ball we'll be attending at the end of the week." Lucas seemed to catch her flinch. "TCO is putting it on for the American Red Cross. It's an annual event. Don't worry though, stylists will take care of you. And you won't have to do a thing but what comes naturally— charm every guest there."

Even with her shy sense of reluctance, she couldn't say no to charity.

Would this be her life from now on? Parties, public engagements, marble floors that looked too fancy to actually walk on?

Dear Lord, she wasn't a socialite. She wasn't a billionaire's typical choice in women....

"Alicia," he said, touching her arm.

Her body came alive. But she couldn't allow him to see how afraid she was, how out of her element.

"I'm in an adjustment period." Her smile was shaky.

"Me, too." He took her hand, engulfing her much smaller one in warmth and reassurance. "You're freaked out and I understand that. But I'm convinced that you were meant to be my wife, even if we've got a long way to go before we know each other fully. Having you and Gabe here with me makes this penthouse someplace I want to come home to, Alicia. It was lacking the both of you and I never realized it. If I'd traveled back here without you…"

His grip tightened around her fingers as he glanced away. The slight, chilled wind huffed at his hair, and a muscle in his jaw twitched.

Was he choked up or something? Alicia squeezed his

hand, profoundly touched. So happy to have found what God had always meant for her: People to take care of and treasure. A situation she could depend on to keep her and Gabriel emotionally secure. A predictable pattern to her days that would cover the doubts about her true self.

He cleared his throat but still didn't meet her gaze. "It's been a long day, but there's so much to talk about, like ways to help Gabe adjust, too."

"I know things have gone quickly, but we've got a lot of time to work everything out now."

Married. The reality of that sent a twinge of carnal hunger over her skin.

Instinctively, she slid her thumb over his, an invitation she couldn't take back.

He seemed to stop breathing.

What did she want him to do? Kiss her? Slip his hands under her clothing and coax every piece off her body?

She wanted it and…and she didn't. Lord, help her, she was terrified of what she might find within herself.

When he covered her hand with both of his, she knew he'd seen her panic. Great. Some hot-tamale wife she'd be, he was probably thinking.

"You look nervous enough to jump out of your skin."

He seemed bothered by this, as if something was eating at him from the inside out.

"It's fine, but I… I'm…"

"You're not ready." He laughed, the sound edged with frustration. "I suspected as much—not that I blame you. You're more innocent than ninety-nine percent of the adult population, and I'll bet you're used to more of a courtship than the one you got."

She didn't say anything, even though she should've told him right then and there that she wasn't as pure as he believed.

At her silence, he shook his head. "Listen, how about we…" He laughed again. "I don't know…start our official honeymoon phase in…well, a week?"

A week? Was he serious? He wasn't going to demand anything until then?

He was being more understanding than she could've ever guessed, and, in a way, that unbalanced her. But what had she expected him to be? A caveman or a gentleman?

She thought, once again, of the man who'd offered her his coat to cover up her wet blouse and she knew the answer without a doubt.

She scanned his features, they were shaded with something like guilt. Did he feel badly because she was having such a hard time here?

"You'd put everything off until I…"

"Get used to me? Yeah." He let go of her hands and shrugged, a slant of shadow otherwise hiding his reaction. "This just gives me one more week to romance you, right? A week we need to get everything to normal before we can relax."

"These past few days have been very emotional…" Oh, *Dios*, she felt as if a boulder had been lifted off her chest. She still couldn't believe he was being so giving, but thank goodness for it.

"No apologies. I've told you before and I meant it—I'm just happy you agreed to be with me."

Then, noticing that she was shivering in earnest now, he said, "Come on," leading her back inside, up the spiral staircase and to the third floor, where their grand bedroom awaited. Beyond the thick wooden doors, a canopy hovered over the massive bed, low lights dusking the paneled walls and setting the scene for a wedding-night ritual that would be delayed—just until she got her bearings, she told herself. Just until then.

Softly, he kissed her on top of her head, his breath labored and warm against her hair.

Her pulse felt like taps of rain on a metal roof that was held up by brittle poles. She almost wished there would be a next move, nearly dreading it, wanting it so badly that it was pulling her apart.

When he stepped away from her and headed toward the door, the world seemed to collapse.

"Sleep well," he said softly, his eyes dark and unreadable. He paused, as if wanting to say something else, as if wanting to stay. But he didn't.

No, he just closed the door behind him, leaving her standing there for what seemed like an hour.

It'd been so easy for him to leave her alone on their honeymoon night and, even though it made her feel so much better, it also made things so much worse.

Didn't he want her enough to persuade her?

In the darkness, her confusion raged. One week, she thought.

One week until she had to face her demons all over again.

* * *

"You're going to give me the rundown on our biggest clients then?" Lucas asked an assistant the next day in TCO headquarters.

Barnaby, a slim man with a hundred-dollar haircut and an ambitious suit, made a weary face. During the last hour, Lucas had found that the guy wasn't much for holding back snarky comments, but, somehow, that was kind of refreshing.

Just like Alicia.

"I don't get promotions by filing my nails all day, Mr. Chandler," the assistant answered.

Made sense, Lucas thought. And *he* wouldn't move ahead, either, by staying away from the office. So he'd embarked upon phrase three of the Respect Plan— getting to know his own company.

As both of them strolled through the fortieth-floor lobby, a redheaded receptionist, one he couldn't recall ever meeting whether it was at a social event or just in passing, winked at him. The old Lucas would've veered right over to her, pursuing her sly invitation. But the new one?

He thought of his wife's golden eyes, her beautiful smile.

The new Lucas didn't have any interest in flirting with anyone else. Strange, what a life mission could do to a guy.

And that's all this was, Lucas thought. A crusade to change the playboy reputation, even if it meant running five miles in the gym every day to let off some sexual steam.

He was going to do right by Alicia, even if everything had started off wrong.

As they entered Lucas's pristine office, he lackadaisically clumped his briefcase on the empty desk near a state-of-the-art computer system that he would be using to research TCO.

Barnaby would be key to this. David told him that he'd assigned the assistant to be Lucas's number-one man because, in spite of his pointed wit, he'd proven himself to be a lion tamer who knew how to whip a situation into shape. But Lucas suspected that David had foisted Barnaby on him out of pure competitive spirit, just to make sure his entry into the world of business wasn't too smooth.

Nonetheless, he was here to make sure that his dad noticed his life turnaround, right along with the rest of the planet. It hadn't been easy to ignore the derogatory looks he'd received upon entering the office, the doubtful raised brows and snickers that had trailed him. But he was here. He was ready.

"Anything else you need from me right now?" Barnaby asked.

Yeah, Lucas thought. *Tell my wife that I'm sorry about leaving her alone on our wedding night.*

But he knew delaying the sex was wise—she clearly wasn't ready, yet, and he couldn't stomach the idea of forcing the issue.

So, instead of waking up as a satisfied groom, he'd tumbled out of his own bed, then gone to TCO at the crack of dawn. But, before leaving, he'd made a point to stop by Gabe's room to touch his cheek, to make sure he was really there.

"I think you've got enough to do, for now," Lucas told Barnaby, going to the other side of his desk to sit. As he sank into the leather, he caught a glimpse of the gray, bustling city outside the window, the scatter of a thousand other businesspeople who were doing what they had to do for survival.

"Yes, Mr. Chandler. I'll be chained to my desk until midnight if you need anything else."

"Barnaby."

At the sternness of Lucas's tone, the assistant raised an eyebrow, as if unaccustomed to being challenged. Or maybe everybody at TCO, including Barnaby, didn't think enough of the wild Chandler child to offer any respect.

"We can work one of two ways," Lucas said evenly. "You can launch verbal missiles and I can bat them down every minute of the day until I get tired of it and fire you. Or you can treat me like your boss and eventually end up as a right-hand man to the guy who already owns the majority of this company." He leaned forward, his hands clasped on the desk. "Decide now."

For a long second, Barnaby didn't move. But then, with a small grin, he said, "Welcome to your first day of work, Mr. Chandler. I'll be at my desk."

He turned around and Lucas let out a subtle breath. One down, hundreds to go.

But before the assistant exited, he turned around. "And congratulations on your marriage and the adoption. From the press she's already gotten, Mrs. Chandler seems like a very sweet woman." He raised the eyebrow again. "Just imagine—a new wife who wants to put off her own honeymoon so she can get the household in order. I myself don't know many ladies who would be that giving."

He was referring to the story in today's *Post*, a throwaway line that explained why Lucas hadn't swept Alicia off to somewhere exotic already. But the gleam in Barnaby's eyes said that he wasn't convinced the playboy had been erased, even though none of the TCO employees outside of family were privy to the stunt marriage.

Perceptive, Lucas thought as Barnaby left. He would need people like that on his side if he was going to succeed.

He ran a hand over his empty desktop, realizing again that there wasn't anything pressing for him to work on, that he didn't know what was going on with his company at all.

But, even worse, he had to admit that he didn't know what was happening with the woman he'd left sleeping in a separate bedroom in their home.

His own wife.

The stylist—a woman named Tatiana who wore her hair in a slashing, sophisticated cut—finally left the penthouse, and Alicia sank to the thick carpet.

In front of her, a cinema-sized TV was flashing a Disney movie; it'd been entertaining Gabriel throughout most of the appointment and, during all the fitting and measuring, Alicia had been restless to get back to him.

She didn't like using the tube as a babysitter. She

also didn't like perusing the list of nanny candidates Lucas had faxed over earlier.

The echo of an animated lion cub's roar bounced off the walls, the fancy artwork, the exquisite trim.

Looking at the opulence, Alicia shrank into herself.

This place was so foreign, so unlike her. Did Gabriel feel the same way?

Not judging by the way he was focused on the movie. But maybe that was because he knew she was here and she wasn't ever going to leave him. Maybe that's what made all the difference.

Yet, couldn't she say the same about Lucas? Shouldn't she feel secure because he would always be there, too?

"Ready for a snack, Gabriel?" she asked, trying to get her head back in a more comfortable place.

The child flinched, as if just realizing she was in the same room. Glancing behind him, he smiled. "Hi, Miss Alicia," he said in a chirpy voice, ignoring her question.

Then, turning back to the TV, he reabsorbed himself in the animation. A child's world.

"You can call me Mama now, Gabriel," she said softly, knowing he probably couldn't hear her. But she wanted to voice it, to make it real.

He didn't answer.

Well, perhaps she could talk to him more when she had his full attention. Let him enjoy a cartoon for a while.

Still, she scooted forward, touching Gabriel's back.

He was so tiny, made of skin and bones and the heart of a little boy who needed so much protection and love.

Or maybe she was the one who needed it at the moment. She thought back to the stylist's appointment.

"Now, that's *you*," the stranger named Tatiana had said, pen poised over a clipboard as she adjusted her cat-eye glasses with her free hand.

Alicia still felt uneasy at the memory. Tatiana had dressed her in a tight black sheath by some supposedly hot designer. It clung to the ample curves she'd always tried to hide under loose clothing. The décolletage dipped low, exposing much more cleavage than Alicia had ever dared.

"With the right jewelry and shoes, you'll be acceptable," Tatiana had said, marking her checklist of things to buy.

Smarting from the comment, Alicia had watched herself in the full-length stand-alone mirror they'd set up near the TV and Gabriel. She hadn't been able to move, more aware than ever of how she really didn't fit in, with her toasty skin, her gauche posture.

But none of that seemed to matter to Lucas.

She'd run her hands over her hips. What would he think? Would he be able to resist her now?

But… Absently, she'd touched her bracelet. The silver was cold. Plus, the price tag on this dress probably reflected enough money to pay for the comfort of three orphans for one whole year.

"This just isn't me," she'd told Tatiana, who'd tried to talk her back into buying the dress.

But Alicia had insisted on a more conservative wardrobe, even when it came to the design for the gown that would be tailored for the charity ball.

At that point, she'd felt more isolated than ever. She'd sunk into an invisible hole, hollowed out by the same mortification that had encouraged her abstinence vows.

What would Lucas do if he found out she wasn't what he thought she was—a woman capable of making him a better man? How was she qualified for that when she'd been born at the opposite end of the moral spectrum?

His angel, she thought. If only he knew better.

Then it occurred to her. Was she so much of an angel that he didn't *want* to sleep with her and that's why he hadn't made more of an issue of it? Had she married a man with a Madonna complex in her haste to find her dream?

Unsettled, she gave a final pat to the engrossed Gabriel's back, then stood. She wasn't sure what to do with herself and that threw her off because she'd never felt so at a loss before.

Wanting to remain near her son—her son; how many times would she have to think it to believe it?—she gingerly sat in an overstuffed white leather chair and hoped it wouldn't be ruined by the time she got up. Then, fidgety, she looked around, saw a pile of newspapers that Ms. Boland had dropped off this morning on a nearby table and grabbed one.

As Gabriel's movie played on, she leafed through the *New York Post*.

But a certain large full-color picture made her pause.

In it, she and Lucas were in front of his private jet, arms around each other as he nuzzled her forehead.

Gabriel was looking up at his new father as if Lucas were the end-all-be-all, while the billionaire cupped the child's head in a loving gesture.

She remembered that moment, when a spark of happiness in her chest had met the flash of a reporter's camera.

Then her gaze traveled lower. "The Playboy Takes a Wife!" read the headline.

Tears threatened to bully her, so she held them in. The unread paper crackled as she strangled it.

But she couldn't lose composure. Not in front of Gabriel. Never in front of her son.

In the foyer, she heard a door close and she fought to put herself back together.

At first, Lucas didn't see Alicia sitting near the back of the room. He'd heard the TV even from the foyer and, judging from the bippity-dippity sounds, he'd known it was something Gabe would be watching.

When he saw the kid sitting in front of the home-theater screen, he dive-bombed him, so relieved to finally be out of the office and in a place where he could relax.

"There he is!" he said, scooping up the boy and lifting him.

Gabe squealed, widened his eyes, then spread out his hands as if he were flying. "Man!"

Swinging the kid back down and holding him, Lucas said, "Remember our talks? I'm your daddy now."

Alicia had translated many of those discussions because Gabe couldn't possibly understand the subtleties in English. Lucas even doubted he would understand them in Spanish, but this was something that had to be addressed. Every day, if need be.

Gabe seemed to latch on to the word *daddy*. He brightened up even more, pointing to Lucas's chest. "Daddy?"

"*Sí.* Yes. Daddy."

Those five letters spread through him, warming him through and through. He hugged Gabe, enjoying the feel of how the boy clung to him. He'd never experienced anything like it before, not in a drag race, a free fall or even with his own brother.

"Where's your mom?" When Gabe didn't answer, Lucas tried again, dying to see her. "Mama? Miss Alicia—but we call her Mama now."

"I'm here," said a small voice from behind him.

Blood jerking in his limbs, Lucas turned to her. Her smile was wide yet oddly stiff, and she was back to wearing her shapeless orphanage clothes. They paled next to the white leather and elegant decor. In fact, she looked out of place and tiny, dwarfed by the magnitude of her surroundings.

But to Lucas, she belonged.

She seemed to be the center of everything.

He thrust the rogue notion away. TCO was the axis that held his world together. Alicia and Gabe were business.

Just business.

When Gabe squirmed, Lucas put him down to go back to his movie, then approached Alicia, noticing that the corners of her mouth twitched, as if her smile were about to fail.

"I didn't get the chance to tell you goodbye this morning," he said, unable to voice what was really bugging him.

She nodded, her knuckles going white as she linked her fingers together in her lap.

"Alicia…"

Her smile finally fell. "I'm afraid I'm not handling all these changes very well."

Don't touch her, his callous side said. *Don't get closer than you have to in order to make this work.*

But he couldn't help himself.

He bent down, cupped the back of her neck. "What can I do?"

When she glanced up at him with those beautiful golden eyes, there were questions rather than answers.

What am I doing here?

How do I handle being your wife?

His heart lurched. He couldn't allow things to implode now. Not when he'd already come so far.

He knew what was needed. He just had to win her over again, right? That's all there was to it.

"You know what would be fun?" he asked.

She looked doubtful that anything could be fun. "What?"

He thought of their picnic under the oak tree, their Wiffle-ball game, and hoped she was remembering those days, too.

With a playful smile he didn't even have to summon, he gently nicked her under the chin. "How about I surprise you?"

And, when her own smile emerged—a real yet tentative one this time—he drew her out of the chair.

Determined to make this work.

Chapter Nine

With all the personal upheaval, Alicia had almost forgotten it was December, a time of year she normally loved, with all the carols on the radio, the fun of buying presents and the anticipation of a Christmas feast.

How had Lucas known that he could cheer her up just by reminding her of the holidays? she wondered while her little family, dressed in heavy coats, gloves and knit hats, stood in front of the Christmas tree at Rockefeller Center. It rested in grandeur over a rink of colorfully garbed skaters, as well as a lighted angel that was shining in the early evening's darkness.

Being here made Alicia want to sing and thank God for this wonderful opportunity she'd been given. Today, she'd just forgotten how lucky she was, that's all.

Lucas provided a reminder when he'd first taken her and Gabriel to Toys "R" Us, where their son had tirelessly explored the wonderland of toys and, at the same time, given her ideas for his gifts. Then Lucas had ushered them to the breathtaking holiday windows of Saks Fifth Avenue. After they'd gawked at the intricate tableau, he'd urged them inside the store, telling them to pick out whatever they wished. Money was no object.

Alicia couldn't quite get used to that philosophy as she helped Gabriel choose his own clothing. The salespeople had been patient as the child had flitted from one rack to another, too active to try anything on. Ultimately, while Lucas had entertained Gabriel by going up and down the crowded escalators with him, she'd selected a few winter outfits, even though the price tags had floored her.

Afterward, they'd come to the Christmas tree, and both Gabriel and Alicia had been swept up in the spectacle.

Amidst the spirited throng in the plaza, Lucas—the only one hardy enough to brave the chill without a hat—was holding Gabriel so he could get a better view of the skaters.

"Flying!" the little boy said, pointing a mittened hand at a young girl as she whizzed by, her scarf floating behind her.

"You want to skate, too?" Lucas asked the child. Then he turned to Alicia. "I can arrange admission."

Just then, a big man in a red jacket crashed to the ice in an amazing spill. The onlookers collectively recoiled and went, "Ooh."

Gabriel emphatically shook his head. "No want to skate."

When Alicia reached out and patted the child in sympathy, she laughed, her breath coming out in a plume of smoke. Gabriel was instantly amused. He giggled and imitated her, creating his own puckered clouds.

"Blowing smoke sure beats entertaining the masses with *my* skating skills," Lucas said drily.

As Gabriel kept huffing, Alicia said, "You sound relieved that the activity was ixnayed."

"I am." He chuckled, squeezing Gabriel, who laughed. "Believe me, I'd rather take part in sports that don't highlight sequins and spandex during competition."

"That's right, we don't want to chip away at your machismo." She'd heard about his racing cars and foolhardy derring-do. "Unless you could get killed before you cross a finish line, you're not into it."

At first, he seemed surprised at her lighthearted teasing. Heck, she was a little taken aback by it, too, but Christmas in the air had made her feel free, happy.

Then he nodded, his grin wry. "I won't ever be into that sort of thing again, Alicia. Those days are long gone."

Good. She didn't relish the idea of a husband who took part in freewheeling activities that could easily kill him. "Long gone?"

"Yeah." Lucas smiled at Gabriel as the child clapped his hands at a woman who was spinning on the ice like a graceful toy top. "After my father's health scare, I realized that I hadn't lived up to any of his expectations, and that didn't sit right with me. So one of the first things I did in my effort to change was cut out the daredevil stuff."

With a start, it hit her—she really knew so little about this man. She'd been so busy focusing on the benefits for Gabriel and her own craving for family that this small detail had been swept under the carpet.

Impetuousness, her cautious side said. *See? You're paying a price for it now.*

Apparently sensing a change in her, Lucas turned from the ice rink, leading them away as he threaded a path through the thick crowd and got out his cell phone to call their driver.

She took the opportunity to piece together everything she did know about her husband. In the days before the wedding, during the few short conversations they'd had, he'd mentioned a few more details about his relationship with David, as well as his dad's close call with death. But it was only now that she was even beginning to comprehend what sort of effect Ford Chandler's near demise had really visited on Lucas.

At the thought of meeting her father-in-law tomorrow at dinner, she blew out a breath. It iced the air like a ghost.

They ambled back toward Saks, where they would be picked up. In one arm, Lucas held Gabriel and, with the other, he reached back for Alicia so they could link hands and dodge all the other people on the sidewalk together.

Even through her glove she felt his skin blaze against hers.

When they were ensconced in the limo and Gabriel

was busy looking at a new cloth picture book about tug-boats, Alicia glanced at Lucas sitting opposite her.

"Your father," she said. "You must care about him a lot if he got you to change your lifestyle."

A muscle ticked in his jaw as he nodded.

His dad was obviously a touchy subject, so she tread lightly. "Since he was too sick to come to our wedding, I wonder what he thinks about us? Is he unhappy that it happened so quickly? I mean, maybe he wanted you to settle down, but will he believe you rushed into it just as you, the daredevil, rushed into a lot of other things?"

He laughed, and it wasn't with any joy.

"Don't worry—he supports the kinder, gentler me. But still…" They were stuck in traffic, so his gaze was trained on the buildings visible through the window. "I think the Chandlers own a quarter of these properties. *That's* what my dad is proud of. That's the bottom line."

The emptiness of his words saddened her. "I'm sorry."

"Don't be. My dad's a first-class ba—" He stopped himself. "Beg your pardon—jerk. But you have to be ruthless in business, I suppose. At least, that's what I'm learning."

"Learning?"

"For the first time today, I spent more than one hour in TCO headquarters."

Oh. Really? "I don't understand. I thought you were an important part of the company."

"Not before my dad's stroke. Along with this whole life makeover, I decided to actually get my hands dirty doing something other than playing in the sandbox.

The odd thing is, I'm pretty sure I fit into TCO about as well as I do with my dad and mom."

"Which isn't much?"

He finally faced her head-on. "Which isn't much."

Leaning forward, she wrapped her fingers around his. Words weren't needed, not when she understood the canyon between child and parents so keenly, herself.

Gabriel chose that moment to bolt up in his seat, tossing the book away. "Toooooot, toooooot!" he said, imitating the tugboats in the pictures.

As if thankful for the reprieve, Lucas held her hand tighter, then grinned, pulling his son to his side. The child laughed, always up for having a good time with his adored idol.

All through the rest of the ride, through the trip in the elevator up to their penthouse, through a catered dinner from a restaurant down the street that Alicia honestly wished to have cooked herself, instead, she felt it—a strengthened connection with her husband. A ferocity to make him happy because that's what he'd done for her today just when she'd been at her lowest.

But after they tucked in Gabriel and it was bedtime for them, too, Lucas settled at the dining table to look over some paperwork he'd brought home.

Today, she'd realized how much of a stranger he really was.

Less than one week until I become a real wife to a man I barely know, she thought. *Just a matter of days.*

She retreated into herself, once again the woman

who had avoided sex for years—the woman who was perhaps even afraid of having it.

Quietly she went to her cold bed, listening for the sounds of her husband retiring to his own room a half hour later.

Wishing, in spite of everything, that he would've come to her, instead.

After another day at work—one filled with so much research about TCO that Lucas's head was set to explode—he found himself rushing home. Alicia met him in the foyer, already dressed for dinner with his father.

The oxygen gushed out of him.

She wore just slightly more makeup than usual, with pink lipstick and a bit of blush. Her dark curls were pinned up and, in cameo softness, tendrils brushed the rose-and-black lace shawl that covered her shoulders. A black dress floated down to her suede pumps, the sleeves long, yet sheer.

Damn, she was a woman who seemed to have no idea just how gorgeous she was in her classy ensemble.

"Wow," was all he could say.

"I…" She shrugged, then tugged at her skirt as if it were too tight. "Tatiana, the stylist, picked it out. Someone also came in to do my makeup, even though I'm perfectly capable."

Unable to help himself, he sauntered toward her. Slowly, he kissed her hello, wishing again that she would've forgotten all about the postponed honeymoon and invited him into her room last night.

He sipped at her, tasting lipstick and sweetness. Not caring that he was ruining the makeup job.

Leaning into him, she seemed to both perk up and relax.

"You look like a million bucks," he said against her mouth.

She pulled away slightly, her breath warm on his lips even at this tentative distance. "I do?"

"Hell, yeah. I mean, *heck,* yeah." He rested his fingers at her neck, stroking his thumb there, trying to keep her from backing away even more. "My father's probably going to wonder why he didn't find you first, the old goat."

She made a surprised face and he laughed. "It's a joke. You know—serial husband? Remember?"

"I remember." After a pause, she seemed to gather her wits, then started to help him off with his long coat. "So how was work, *honey?*"

He chuckled at the abrupt teasing, trying to keep his frustrations in check. "Well, my assistant, Barnaby, could enter the Snippy Race in the Olympics and take home the gold, but…" He shrugged. "Other than that? Still not great."

"Why?"

He hesitated, weighing the idea of keeping her in the dark about everything, not just this relationship. It'd be so much easier never to tell her what he'd done, but more and more, he kept thinking he needed to do it.

Yeah, right. That'd be perfect, he thought. *Alienate your wife and ruin the good thing you have going. Just*

shut up and she'll never know the difference, okay?
Shut up and just make her happy.

But she was his *wife* now. He liked the thought of
her being interested enough to want to ask about the
reasons work could've gone better today. Liked the
thought of being honest with her.

So he went halfway, at least, telling her about how
the junior executives smirked whenever he asked them
questions about their projects. He told her how, today,
David had "forgotten" to give him the time of a meeting
with the top-rank players in the company. His truthful-
ness felt good, but he knew this was as far as he dared
go with it.

"David can't do that." Alicia looked pissed enough
for both of them. It lifted him up knowing that someone
was on his side.

She continued, walking with him through the foyer
and toward the common area. "You've told me before
that you're the majority stockholder."

"Right."

"So why does David feel justified in walking all
over you?"

Because I'm the face. I've never been anything even
remotely resembling the brains of TCO.

It was too sad—too embarrassing—to admit.

As they entered the common area, Gabe saved
him by popping up from behind a couch and yelling,
"Man!"

Okay, he wasn't always saying "Daddy," but that
would come someday, Lucas supposed.

"Get over here!" He held out his arms, latching on

to the flying boy and swishing him into the air as the kid squealed.

In the background, one of their housekeepers, Mrs. Carillo, stood, her hands filled with plastic toys. She'd obviously been keeping Gabe occupied while Alicia got ready.

"Hi, Mrs. Carillo," he said while Gabe pulled at his ear.

"Mr. Chandler." She nodded to Alicia, then disappeared.

"Magdelena loves playing with Gabriel," Alicia said. "I even talked her into babysitting him tonight since I don't want to leave him with some random stranger."

"Who would?" Lucas dipped his son, increasing the volume of Gabe's gaiety. He lifted him again, succumbing to laughter, too. "Maybe we should hire *her* to help you with Gabe all day."

Uh-huh, he thought. That would go over real well with the social set. Nannies were trophies and the more credentials they came with, the better. He could imagine the raised eyebrows a housekeeper-turned-nanny would inspire.

But he kind of liked the thought of tweaking everyone's noses like that.

"Hire Mrs. Carillo?" Alicia said. "I actually like to spend all day with Gabriel."

Lucas thought of all the plans he'd had for his wife: Hostessing charity benefits, showing her off to the press as the woman who'd turned the playboy around. When would she find time to do that if she didn't get some help with Gabe?

But, as much as it pained him to admit it, he didn't want his new son to ever think he was being shuffled off for an extended amount of time. He would have to be an ogre to do that to the boy.

Lowering Gabe so he could take off for the toys Mrs. Carillo hadn't cleaned up yet, Lucas fixed his gaze on Alicia.

"You'll need a rest every once in a while because Gabe could tire out an army. Why not let him have two people to play with—you and Mrs. Carillo?"

"Three," she added. "You seem to be doing pretty well in the play department when you get home from work."

Really? Lucas had never expected to be decent at it. Maybe Alicia had been right when she'd told him he was meant to be a father. Or maybe she just had no idea what he had up his sleeve.

Stricken with remorse, he clammed up, loosening his tie and walking away so he wouldn't have to face the woman he was betraying.

"I'll be ready to go in fifteen minutes," he said, leaving his family behind without a second glance.

Even though he was dying to look back at them.

Alicia knew that arrangements had been made to buy out the city's trendiest new restaurant for this first meeting with Ford Chandler.

Betheney, which Lucas told her had been named for the wife of the celebrity chef and owner, was decorated with Spanish flair: dusky red-and-beige paintings of flamenco dancers, a mahogany bar and candlelit tables, filigreed screens separating the limited tables. It would hold only twenty-six diners and promised a magnificent experience.

As Alicia walked into the establishment on her husband's arm, she was once again overwhelmed—and it wasn't just because of the riches. There were about ten people here, and she'd only been expecting David and Mr. Chandler. Interestingly, Lucas seemed surprised to see some of them, too, and she wondered why.

She was also worried about Gabriel. Before leaving the penthouse, both she and her husband had sat him down to tell him where they were going for the next few hours. She hadn't known what to expect, predicting that perhaps the child she knew so well would feel abandoned and throw a tantrum. But Gabriel had already taken to Mrs. Carillo and he'd transitioned into the babysitting part of the night without a fuss.

Still, Alicia had her cell phone on just in case.

In the meantime, she was determined to make a positive impression on her father-in-law, a man who'd taken on gargantuan proportions in Alicia's mind.

Ford Chandler greeted her right away, using the aid of a cane. When he took her hand and kissed the back of it, she could see a little bit of Lucas in him. It wasn't his height or the way his silver hair didn't want to go with the flow of how it'd been combed, it was more in the gaze—a predator's violet shine.

"My son told me you were beautiful," he said, his speech slightly slurred by the aftermath of his stroke, "but you surpass that, Alicia." He was still holding her hand.

Lucas nimbly removed it from his father's grasp. "Yeah, she's a keeper. That's why I married her."

Mr. Chandler gave his son a veiled look that Alicia couldn't begin to translate, then turned back to her. "We're overjoyed to have you in our family, and I regret I couldn't make it to the wedding." Something in his eyes went hazy, as if that sentiment had been genuine. "But I am looking forward to talking with you more."

"Gabriel's looking forward to meeting you this weekend, too," she added, even though her son had expressed no such thing. It sounded like something a new wife should say, though.

"And I'm excited about that, as well." Her father-in-law smiled, but she wasn't sure what he was actually feeling. "I can't quite believe I've got a grandson now."

David, who was in the corner chatting with the other guests over drinks, waved at Lucas. Alicia felt him stiffen.

Why did this seem more like a business meeting than a family dinner?

Or was this how all the Chandler gatherings went?

Based on Lucas's feelings about his brood, Alicia thought she knew the answer.

"Dad," he said, "why don't we take a seat."

The older man gritted his teeth, glanced at Alicia, then covered with another smile. "I'm out of the sick bed and hardly an invalid. I can tolerate a little standing."

"Then, I guess you won't mind if I introduce my wife to David's friends." Lucas took her elbow and, even though his touch was gentle, there was a grip to it. "Whoever they are."

"We thought we'd invite the Tadmere group."

Tadmere? Sounded like business to her, all right.

A tight laugh escaped her husband, and he started to lead her away. But not before Mr. Chandler got in one last comment.

"Just look at you, Lucas," he said, his smile wobbling a little.

When his eyes went a softer shade of blue, she realized that this man was surrendering to his son in a very subtle way. A father who was trying to reach out, whether Lucas knew it or not.

From the way her husband remained stiff, she wasn't sure.

Ford sighed, as if acknowledging he wasn't getting anywhere. "I suppose my congratulations wouldn't mean much."

"They might," Lucas said, "if you meant it."

Why wouldn't he? Was there something going on she wasn't aware of?

Without another word, Lucas guided her away, leaving Mr. Chandler to make his slow way back to the table, his hors d'oeuvres and beverage. There wasn't much distance from one end of the room to the other, and Lucas seemed intent on taking his time to get her to the other guests.

"Sorry about this," he said between clenched teeth.

"The lack of intimate family time?"

"That, plus all my dad's 'beautiful' talk. Not that he wasn't right—" here Lucas slid his arm around her waist, making her skin flush "—but I don't want to hear my dad saying stuff like that."

Is this what had been bothering Lucas back there? That's all? "No harm done."

"So you say." He stopped her about fifteen feet away from David and his crowd, turning to her and clasping her elbows so their arms connected like two fortified bridges. "Listen, you need to know what's going on—as far I can tell, anyway. Tadmere is a media-savvy company TCO is trying to acquire, but there are some... difficulties."

Lucas took a deep breath, then paused. What was wrong?

"Like what?" she asked.

"You don't want to know the details." His grip on her grew a little tighter. "Just be your charming self, okay? The hostess who spun me for a loop the first time I saw her."

Lucas warmed inside. He wasn't lying. Alicia had turned his world upside down immediately, and he'd never gotten over it. In fact, if he admitted it, he was still reeling, especially right now, with his arms pressed to hers.

She blushed at the compliment, even if he hadn't come right out and told her he loved her. And he wouldn't. That was one lie he couldn't bear.

"I'm ready when you are," she said, lifting her chin and smiling at him in confederacy.

Alicia, the perfect wife. The smartest choice he'd ever made. His father seemed to agree with that, and it had confused Lucas even more.

Had the old man been coming around back there or

was he just playing with Lucas? He'd seemed sincere when he'd complimented Alicia and maybe he'd even held out a white flag, but their history was too full of hard feelings for Lucas to give in that easily.

Alicia had taken his hand, nudging him toward David and their guests. From Lucas's research, he was familiar with a couple of faces—the owners, a brother and sister who were resisting the sale of Tadmere to TCO because of Lucas's reputation. But the others, all men who seemed to be of Latin persuasion from the gist of their conversation, were a mystery to him.

Why had David invited them?

During a discussion in which Alicia requested a club soda from the waiter and proceeded to charm everyone with her answers to their questions regarding Refugio Salvo, Lucas noticed how the crowd warmed up to her. She had social talent, and David had been right on target when he'd noticed her potential.

Potential that went so much deeper than being a fake wife, Lucas thought, his gut twisting.

As Alicia encouraged the others to talk about their families, David drew Lucas aside, gesturing to the bar and pretending they were going to refresh the nonalcoholic champagne that the Tadmere siblings approved of.

"Da-amn," David said as they set their glasses on the mahogany bar and allowed the waiter to serve them. "How did we get so lucky with her?"

"How did *I* get so lucky?" Lucas grasped his champagne flute's stem so hard that he was shocked it didn't shatter.

"She's incredible. You've got yourself a real—"

"Why are the Tadmeres here? And who is everyone else?"

His brother shrugged. "Second question first—those are Tadmere associates. First question next—Tadmere needs to see up close that you're not the terror they thought you were. And from the way they're enjoying Alicia, you've done good."

He hadn't done any good at all. "Associates of Tadmere? What does that mean, David?"

"Just let me handle everything, Luke. Okay?" With one of those smirks Lucas had seen so much around the office, David said, "Stop with your TCO research and stay home with your family. I've got all this under control."

"Got what under control?" said Alicia's voice.

Both David and Lucas whipped around to find her behind them, frowning. In the background, the guests were being led to the joined tables by the waitstaff, and clearly, Alicia had come over to summon them, too.

"Hi, sis," David said, saluting her with his drink.

Lucas could see some temper in her gaze and he remembered how ticked off she'd been earlier when he'd mentioned how much things sucked at the office. Had she heard David brush him off?

More importantly, just how *much* had she heard?

Panic separated his veins, but when she directed her next comment at David, Lucas calmed down.

"I'm sure you'd find that, if you gave Lucas some respect, he'd be your greatest asset."

Respect. The concept echoed, pierced, shredded.

But he still wanted it. God, did he ever.

David looked amused at her polite feistiness. "Really."

"Oh, yes." Alicia didn't know exactly what they'd been talking about, because she'd only heard David's demeaning tone. But she remembered how angry Lucas had been just about an hour ago when he'd come home from the office and she suspected this conversation had to do with that. "I get the feeling Lucas could do a lot more than anyone gives him credit for."

Out of the corner of her eye, she caught Lucas's smile and she thought that maybe someday he could believe in himself as much as she did.

"Well," David said, straightening up from the bar and smoothing his fancy suit. "This is a perfect match— two people who need to mind their own business."

Taking a sip from his drink, he shot Alicia a meaningful look, then tried to leave.

But not before Lucas grabbed his brother's arm in a gesture that would've looked friendly to a casual observer. Yet to Alicia it was a threat.

"You don't talk to her like that," he said, voice low and dangerous.

David began to laugh, and Lucas gave his arm a tiny shake.

A long beat passed between the brothers before David casually liberated himself and donned a civil grin as he moved toward their guests.

That left them alone. So alone in this room full of strangers.

"What was that…" she began.

Gaze going soft, Lucas smoothed the hair back from her face. "Politics, Alicia. He's sore because I'm infringing on his territory."

"But it's also *your* territory."

"That's right," he said, bending toward her to kiss her forehead. His kisses formed words. *My territory.*

The significance wasn't lost on her as he claimed her with his touch.

A touch that told her just how much he was looking forward to their upcoming honeymoon.

Chapter Ten

Work was a bitch the next day.

David was obviously sore because of how Alicia had stood up to him the night before, so he'd seemed to take great pleasure in diverting Lucas to oversee the charity ball, which was already being handled by a party planner. The message was clear: he was emphasizing Lucas's PR responsibilities instead of inviting him to become a more significant part of running the company.

Yet Lucas was sticking to his guns, bringing home a briefcase full of files that Barnaby had pulled for him: memos and clippings regarding Tadmere.

When he entered the penthouse, the first thing he heard was a Christmas carol coming from the common room. Laughter threaded through the crystalline notes.

Lucas abandoned his briefcase and coat to Ms. Boland, whose brunette hair had mistletoe tucked into its bun.

After he greeted her, he said, "Sounds like there's a party going on."

"You'll see, Mr. Chandler." She smiled, and he realized, maybe for the first time, that this stoic woman who'd always tried so hard to fade into the woodwork—perhaps to avoid his reputed wolfishness and keep her job—was capable of being merry.

Drawn by the warm, festive sounds, Lucas made his way to the common room, lingering in the entrance when he saw what his family was up to.

Next to a bare Christmas tree that waited in the corner, Alicia and Gabe were constructing something of an art project. They'd draped wrinkled earth-toned paper over tables to create rocks and hills, then used simple plastic kitchen wrap to shape a waterfall that tumbled down over some of the "terrain" and into a pool of "water." Fake construction-paper palm trees hovered over that pool.

At the moment, they were working on what looked to be a structure, using bamboo as wood.

Contentment overwhelmed him. Maybe it was the music. Or maybe it was the beginnings of a Christmas tree in a playboy's penthouse—a place that he'd never bothered to decorate in past years. Or maybe it was…

He swallowed, not daring to even think it, because it would go against everything he'd been telling himself about this marriage.

Still, he couldn't stop the longing as he watched his

new family. Gabe looked so comfortable in his new wardrobe, even though his Ralph Lauren pants were missing and he was just running around in his underwear. And Alicia…

She was dressed simply in a white blouse that was untucked, velvet sweat pants and bare feet. Her hair was tied back, curls tumbling past her shoulders.

Once again his hormones revved, spinning in the sand of his frustration. What the hell had he been thinking when he'd put off sex?

Pressure built inside of him, and he almost walked away to remove himself from temptation before it was too late.

But Gabe spotted him, dropping a piece of bamboo and rushing him. "*Es* him!" he said in a hybrid of Spanish and English.

As was their standard greeting, Lucas hefted the boy high above, making him giggle, then held him to his chest, planting a kiss on top of his dark head.

As Lucas's eyes met Alicia's, her face went red, as if a thousand secret fantasies had flooded her at once. He was reminded of the first time they'd met, how she'd seemed bowled over then, too.

Controlling himself, he nodded at the project. "Busy day?"

"Slightly." She brushed her hands together to wipe them off, smiling at him in pure joy. "First, Magdelena said yes to taking care of Gabriel. She'll switch over as soon as Sarah—*Ms. Boland*—hires another personal housekeeper."

First-name basis with all the help? Lucas had always

been cordial with his staff, but now it seemed ridiculous that he'd never called Ms. Boland anything other than that.

"Oh," Alicia added, "and Sarah said something about providing her with a Christmas shopping list?"

"Yeah." Gabe experimentally touched Lucas's nose, and Lucas scrunched it, teasing him. "That'll be taken care of."

"Choosing gifts? Isn't that something we'd like to do?"

He absorbed her confused tilt of the head. Never in his life had he bothered with shopping. Well, there'd been one year, when he'd gotten old enough to believe that Christmas was about giving and all that. But then he'd presented his handpicked gift—a tie clip that he'd purchased from a street cart during a walk with his nanny—to his dad. It hadn't been pretty. In Lucas's little-boy heart, he'd really thought Ford Chandler would love the funky Martian on the cheap metal. But his dad had kind of just flicked it away like a gnat, and that had been the last Lucas had seen of it.

Afterward, he'd gone with the family's personal shopper, too, not having the courage to try again, himself.

But now maybe he did have the guts to buy for his family, especially after the way Alicia had defended him to David last night. He suspected his opinion and effort might just matter to her and Gabe, after all.

"We'll take care of the shopping ourselves, then," he said.

"Excellent." She went up and down on her toes,

hands clasped behind her back. "So…what do you think of the decorations so far?"

He nodded toward the art project, then set Gabe down so the boy could run back to it. "I know what the tree is, but I'm not so sure what's going on in that corner."

She held out her hands in a ta-da motion. "The tree is for you, since you're probably used to one, but I thought we'd bring some Mexico into the place. It's a *Nacimiento.* A Nativity scene."

"Ah." Suddenly the bamboo did seem to be taking the shape of a manger, and he noticed a tiny straw-filled crate by her feet that could double as a baby's bed.

Gabe rattled off some Spanish, then got a baffled look on his face as he glanced at Lucas.

Alicia laughed and answered her son, then spoke to Lucas. "He doesn't know the English for what he said, so I'll translate. He told you that we'll put Baby Jesus in the bed late on *Noche Buena,* Christmas Eve. We normally celebrate on that day and go to mass that night, then eat leftovers on the twenty-fifth. Does that sound good?"

He could only nod, touched that someone would want him to be a part of this.

"And the sixteenth is coming up. It's the beginning of *Las Posadas,* which is traditionally nine days of candlelight processions and festivities. But we'll give it our own personal touch."

Gabe held up a stick of bamboo. *"Feliz Navidad!"*

Lucas smiled. *Feliz Navidad,* indeed. His first happy Christmas. His first inkling of what his life could be like every year if things were different. If he could only open his heart as easily as he'd opened his home.

Ms. Boland appeared from the other room, a camera in hand. "Mr. Chandler, I wondered if you'd like to record this?"

"Photo!" Gabe said, hopping up and down.

Lucas was sick of pictures, flashes that normally captured him for newspapers and magazines, but he wouldn't say no to his son. Besides, this wasn't the press. This was real.

Too real.

He walked past Ms. Boland—Sarah. "Thanks for thinking of it," he said.

"You're welcome, Mr. Ch—"

"It's about time you called me Lucas, all right? Just…Lucas."

As he gathered his family in his arms, pressing his cheek against the softness of his wife's hair and churning with hunger for her, the camera flashed.

And in the viewer that Sarah Boland showed them, Lucas saw a happy family that ripped at his heart.

During Gabe's bedtime, Lucas reclined on the boy's lowered mattress, reading the blanket-bundled child a selection of his favorite books.

Yet after the third Big Bird story, when Gabe tumbled out of bed and picked out a Cookie Monster adventure, Lucas offered another option.

"How about I tell you about the three bears?"

Gabe seemed excited about that, so Lucas shut off the lights, nestled the covers around the kid again and attempted to piece together what he remembered about a plot. It had something to do with a little blond trespasser who pigged out on bear porridge, fell asleep and then…Lucas wasn't sure, but he made it so that the bears adopted Goldilocks just as he and Alicia had adopted Gabe, and that seemed like the best ending anyone could've dreamed up.

He wasn't sure how much the boy liked it, because by the time he was done, Gabe was asleep, his breathing deep and even.

Poor guy, Lucas thought, smoothing back the kid's hair. Worn out from decorating both the Nativity scene, as well as the tree. Lucas had helped, too, and all *he* wanted to do was go to bed. But not alone. Hell, no, not alone.

As if summoned by the beacon of his sexual yearning, Alicia appeared in the doorway, her curvy figure silhouetted by the hall light. Lucas imagined his hands on her hips, her waist, running upward and pressing her into the heat of his body.

Inspired, he crept out of Gabe's toy-strewn room and shut the door. His wife's perfume wafted over him, heady and all-powerful.

Silently, she linked her arm with his, leaning into him as they walked aimlessly. He didn't know where she was leading him, but he could wish it was someplace with a mattress and her body stretched out next to him.

All he knew for sure was that her breast kept brushing against his bicep, and it was driving him crazy.

A few more days, buddy, he thought. *That's all.*

"I've been trying to put together a schedule," she said when they were far enough from Gabe's room so they could talk.

"I've been meaning to get together with you on that."

And so much else. God.

They ended up in the common room, where the lights were out and the Christmas tree was shining with the blue bulbs they'd strung around the branches. The azure glow permeated the area, making it surreal and peaceful.

She sat down on the floor in front of a couch, her back against it, and picked up a gingerbread man that Gabe had been eating earlier. He settled next to her, legs bent, arms resting on his knees.

"The holidays are going to be busy," she said, "so I figured I'd wait to think about another church wedding until afterward."

He remembered how, back in Mexico, he'd promised her a bigger ceremony to make up for the speedy circumstances.

"You just tell me what you need and you've got it," he said. "Speaking of scheduling, you've got your dress and all the trimmings for the charity ball this Friday?"

She sighed a little nervously. "I suppose I'm ready."

"You're going to shine, just like you always do. Don't worry about it."

"Even if the spotlight will be on us? I've seen the tabloids, Lucas. I…"

He touched her hair, and she dropped the gingerbread, then smiled at him in apology. Skittish, he thought. Was she as lit up with desire as he was? Was she wondering if he'd forgotten about his promise to postpone the big night?

"I know—you weren't prepared for everything that came with this marriage. Not yet, anyway." He traced his thumb down her cheek, mesmerized. Soft, so soft. "But, in spite of everything, you're doing a great job."

Business. His tone rang of it. Yeah, she was being the perfect pillar of decency for him. But what was *he* to *her?*

He wasn't sure he wanted to know.

Her breath seemed labored as the quiet enveloped them. When she finally spoke, her voice was croaky.

"How did your day go?"

The change of subject made him drop his hand to the couch.

"All the decorating made me forget to ask," she added.

"I'd rather not have to think about the office when I'm with family, anyway." Not when Gabe and Alicia were turning out to be the only release he had from the stress of TCO. "Work was work, in more ways than one. David was taking petty revenge out on me for my upstart demands to know more about the company. And I think he's still smarting from the way you backed me up."

His heart lifted as he recalled how she'd defended him at Betheney. How it'd seemed so natural for her to do so.

Alicia leaned back against the couch again. The shift in position brought her lips that much closer to his.

"If David doesn't appreciate you," she said, "he needs to know what he's missing."

Lucas tried to laugh, but it was bothering him that

he was keeping her at arm's distance when she was so invested in him. It wasn't right.

His next words slipped out before he could think about what he was doing. "Those unknown guests at dinner last night? I asked David who they were and he told me not to concern myself."

"But you will concern yourself, right?" Even though Alicia knew that Lucas had been more into his daredeviling than TCO in the past, she believed with all her heart that he would be successful at whatever he put his mind to now. He'd done too much for the orphanage for her to doubt his effectiveness. "You're going to look into what's going on around TCO?"

"I guess I was planning on it." Lucas smiled, almost to himself, as if he were treasuring her faith in him. "I brought home more paperwork, thinking I'd get down to the nitty-gritty of something or another."

"Good. That's great, Lucas."

He gave off an aw-shucks aura that captured her. Tremors shivered down her chest, through her belly, humming in a place that she'd been denying for too long.

Suddenly, she was aware of just how close they were sitting, how his skin seemed to vibrate against hers, even if he was inches away. As he turned to her again, his gaze focused on her lips, causing them to tingle.

Ready, she thought. *Maybe I am ready....*

But when he laughed tightly, then turned back toward the tree, she lost any confidence she might have had.

Three more days, thought the side of her that had avoided physical contact for so many years. *The pressure's off for a little while longer.*

Because sex would change everything, especially *her*. It would bring her repressed dark side screaming to life and, now that it was so close, she was less sure than ever that she could handle what would come to the surface. Her father's daughter.

As almost an apology, she leaned her head on Lucas's shoulder, and they both watched the tree. It was such a sweet moment that she wished it would last forever, with no worries, no expectation, no fear that everything wonderful would soon come to an end.

He rested his head against hers. "This is nice," he said softly, voice strangled by something that was part frustration and part…what? An emotion she couldn't identify.

"Nice," she repeated, staring at the lights of their tree.

As he held her hand, she closed her eyes, thinking how much she didn't deserve this husband.

A man who understood her probably even more than she understood herself.

Two shocks awaited Lucas the next morning.

First, it'd been waking up in front of the Christmas tree embracing Alicia, then it'd been temptation at work.

But, at the end of the day, as he rode up in the elevator to the penthouse, he dwelled on the first one more than the other, because his wife had been consuming him for hours.

They'd somehow fallen asleep, silent, wrapped in each other's arms. Upon waking, he hadn't so much as breathed because he hadn't wanted to disturb the adorable pattern of her sleep. She'd felt so good, so innocent against him, and he'd realized that maybe he'd been doing things wrong his whole life.

Holding her made him feel closer than he'd ever been to a woman, and he hadn't even needed sex. Whoa.

But it was true, and that scared the tar out of him because the last thing he needed was to get this close.

Without waking Alicia, he'd carried her to her bed, then tenderly tucked her in and kissed her. It'd taken all his willpower to leave the room, but when he'd done it, he'd felt like a bigger person in some weird way.

He'd gone into work early, before the scent of coffee filled the halls and the click of keyboards interrupted the silence. At quarter after ten—he knew the time because he'd marked it as the moment he'd officially lost his wits—a mergers-and-acquisitions executive he'd previously "dated" had entered his office, congratulated him on his marriage with a disbelieving grin, shut the door and offered him the chance to have his way with her that night.

He'd said no. *No.*

It's not that his body wasn't scrapping for some activity, but he didn't want it from anyone but his wife.

Lucas had no idea how that'd happened. Where was his need to cling to the lifestyle that'd kept him sane for so many years? Wasn't he making himself vulnerable, just as his father had been so many times?

What had happened to his business marriage, for God's sake?

Yet, now, as he entered his home and saw Alicia, everything seemed to coalesce. Nothing mattered but her—not his sanity, the office or even his thwarted libido.

And, when he saw Gabe showing him how he'd learned to somersault at the park today, life seemed complete.

After a home-cooked dinner featuring *chimichangas,* Lucas helped Alicia give Gabe a bath. The boy was in one of his moods, but Lucas and Alicia worked together to calm and discipline him. In between building Nativity scenes and getting the household in order, she'd been interviewing and checking into therapists for their son and, after Gabe retired, they sat at the dining-room table and settled on one.

But now, as darkness peered in the windows, Lucas decided to focus on his research, just to distract himself. Next to him, Alicia created a scrapbook boasting pictures of Gabe.

Still, every few seconds, it seemed, Lucas would look up and take her in, bolstered by the sight of her, knowing that she was there to support him in anything. The notion built him up so high that it felt as if nothing could tear him down.

Funny, he thought, how the last person in the world who should be respecting him actually did.

A confession about how this marriage had come about bucked against his teeth, but he knew everything would crash down around them if he said something. Yet, dammit, he had to tell her. He couldn't live with himself if he didn't.

But…no. Not if he wanted things to stay as they were.

With a start, he realized that he'd become too attached to let her and Gabe go.

Off balance, he went back to a Tadmere global asset

report that Barnaby had put together, attempting to re-cover. And when he came across something that disturbed him even more only fifteen minutes later, Alicia noticed.

"What is it?" she asked.

After only a slight hesitation, he decided to tell her. It was a consolation prize taking the place of everything else.

At the same time… He glanced at the report again, knowing he couldn't tell her every detail about the hor-rific suspicions that were forming in his head.

"Tadmere," he said, throat scratched.

She put down a picture she'd been trimming, as well as the scissors. "What about it?"

He had to be careful. "Well, first off, I've told you that they own a lot of American TV and radio stations. I didn't realize they had some in Mexico. David never told me."

She blinked. "Mexico."

"I can't shake the feeling that David was hiding this information from me, even when he invited those extra guests to dinner the other night." Latin Tadmere execu-tives who, he suspected, had been summoned to see just what a change Lucas had made from playboy to de-voted husband.

With a Latina wife.

He didn't reveal that part because he wasn't sure if he was right about David's intentions. After all, Lucas wasn't a real businessman. And what if he was wrong? That would make him an even bigger joke than he already was.

Besides, how could he explain the doubts that were forming? Doubts that David might have steered Lucas into a relationship with a Latina so TCO could get friendly press in key demographic communities that tuned in to Tadmere stations.

It would devastate her, and that's the last thing Lucas wanted, even if he'd set her up for it in so many ways.

Good God…it would devastate *him*.

"You know," she said, forehead furrowed, "I heard David on the phone once, back in Mexico. He was saying something about a demographic…." She picked up the picture again, avoiding his gaze.

He was about to pursue that comment, but he was afraid to. Yup, the guy who went extreme bungee jumping in New Zealand and drove Formula 1 cars was just plain chicken.

Had David been referring to how Alicia might help with customers from across the border? Had her ethnicity been some sort of selling point with Tadmere?

Or was Lucas just jumping to cynical conclusions because he was paranoid?

For the first time in his life, he wanted to rip David's head off. Not for how he might've manipulated Lucas but for how Alicia had been reduced to a statistic. He wanted to do some damage to himself, too, for getting her into this.

Most of all, he wished he had the courage to tell Alicia everything right now. But he couldn't.

And it wasn't just because he was afraid that the truth might tear this business deal apart.

Chapter Eleven

Finally, Friday, the charity ball arrived.

After kissing Gabriel good-night and letting Magdelena know that they might be back late, Alicia took one of the limos by herself to the Waldorf-Astoria, where she was meeting her husband.

He'd been forced to stay late at work—something to do with David taking a sudden trip to Los Angeles—so she'd messengered one of his tuxes to TCO headquarters. But, before sending it, she'd given in to a whim, pressing her face against the material, smelling it, taking the imagined essence of him into her.

Nighttime fantasies of Lucas were dogging her, as was the niggling feeling that she was missing something important about Tadmere and "demographics."

Worst of all, clock stroke by clock stroke, she was coming to realize that this fear of sex was ruining her more than the act itself ever could. Lucas had never, ever made her feel cheap, so why did she believe making love with him would ruin her?

Alicia was still grappling with her doubts as the limo drew up to the prestigious hotel. While tamping down her nerves, she smoothed her dress, a blush-satin concoction with extended, fashionably buttoned sleeves, an Empire waistline and a chiffon-paneled skirt that flowed down to the pearl-strapped low-heeled slippers she wore. She'd refused the help of the makeup or hair people, whom Sarah Boland had suggested, instead, electing to do everything herself. This, of course, meant that she wasn't wearing much besides blusher, a bit of lipstick, mascara and a simple hairstyle that swept the curls off her neck. Lastly, she wore her charm bracelet, having entwined it with a long strand of pearls around her wrist. It reminded her of who she really was, who she needed to leave behind if she was going to make her marriage work.

All in all, she felt like a girl playing dress-up in Cinderella's ball gown, but she attempted to put that out of her mind. Tonight wasn't about how she looked, it was about TCO raising money for the American Red Cross. She wondered if, someday, she could do the same for orphanages, especially Refugio Salvo. Lucas had been encouraging her to take up philanthropic activities, and, as soon as she arranged their formal wedding, Gabriel's comfort and the household, she would make a great effort to organize her plans.

Before she knew it, her door opened and flashes from the waiting cameras greeted her. For a thin-blooded second she didn't know how to react. Hide because she didn't belong in this dress, in this limo? Or smile because she was now the wife of a man who'd been born into such fame and fortune?

Putting on a false sense of belonging, she stepped onto the red carpet. But then, out of nowhere, a strong hand enveloped hers. She knew the feel of that grip. Lucas.

His warm skin sent a hush of comfort into her, calming her and allowing her to be Alicia Sanchez Chandler, a woman who had every reason to smile.

And she did, beaming, glancing up at him through the flashes. Out of the corner of her eye she caught a peek of the reporters, but when she saw how her husband was gazing at her, she lost all focus except for him.

He looked bowled over at the sight of her, as if he'd never seen a female before. He clasped his free hand lightly over his heart as if to keep it inside his chest.

"Alicia," she heard him say over the camera clicks and the calls from the photographers to look their way for a picture.

At the gritty tenor of his voice, sexual heat rose up from her center and through her body, dabbing her with longing. The sound of him owning her name made her feel innocent and craved all at once, and there was no shame in it at all.

How could she doubt that he valued her, wanted her, celebrated her with every heartbeat that pulsed between them?

I love him, she thought. *I have from the first minute I saw him. He deserves to know exactly who he married, deserves to have me tell him that I'll always be his angel, no matter what he finds out about me.*

No one else on that red carpet seemed to exist as he carefully tucked her hand into the crook of his arm and escorted her into the hotel. She was faintly aware of Art Deco grandeur, marble and flowers suffusing the lobby and halls as they made their way to the gala.

"How was Gabe before you left?" he asked.

She loved that he was thinking of their son instead of the party. "He and Magdelena were playing dress-up, so he was occupied enough to not concentrate on the fact that we won't be there tonight. By the way, he really liked how you called from work to let him know you'd be home later with me." In fact, Lucas made a daily habit of calling from the office, just to tell Gabriel he was on his mind.

Just to tell Alicia he couldn't stop thinking about her, either.

Lucas adjusted his bow tie with his other hand. "He feels comfortable with Mrs. Carillo. Magdelena."

"Very. She's a godsend." Alicia squeezed his arm. "And how about you? Did you get your work done?"

His bicep tensed. "Not quite. I've got something to discuss with David about this Tadmere business, but he took that trip to L.A. and won't return my calls. I stayed a little longer in the office because I was having some meetings with key personnel in order to get even more caught up."

Strange, she thought. Why was David being so cagey?

"Do you trust your brother?" she asked.

Lucas's lips drew into a thin line before he answered. "I used to. Implicitly. But…"

Not anymore. It was easy to supply that answer.

"Hey," he said, lightly nicking her under the chin and shooting her that killer smile. "Why're we talking about TCO when I've got a fairy princess on my arm?"

She melted right then and there.

At that, he got a very translatable look: intense, hungry, his glance brushing her mouth. He started bending toward her, and the music from the ballroom swelled.

"I won't be able to focus in there," he said, his breath whispering over her lips. "I won't be able to think about anything except you."

And as his mouth covered hers, her brain went dark, blanked by everything but the sensation of a moist, warm kiss.

Why wait until tomorrow night? she thought. *I want my husband. I'll have my husband.*

Her lips sent that message and, when he disengaged and cupped her face in his hands to gaze at her, she knew he understood.

They'd finally made it into the ballroom after a rush of guests interrupted their kiss outside. But, now, as Lucas absently listened to a Chandler executive teasing him about how the company playboy had been invaded by a hardworking clone, he couldn't feel any pride at this evidence of the respect he'd been striving for.

No, he couldn't think beyond Alicia.

Had she wordlessly invited him into her bedroom tonight?

Unable to stop himself, he looked around for her again. She'd already done him proud, fitting in with this do-gooder crowd and talking charity with several younger prominent, liberal socialites in the room. With the snootier WASPs, it would take longer for her to be accepted, if ever. He hated to subject her to their type of behavior, but if anyone could handle their bitchery gracefully, it was Alicia. She might even end up changing their outdated attitudes, too.

He scanned the crisp white sculptures of the charitable winter wonderland. It was decorated so that icicles seemed to drift from the ceiling. Fake downy snow dusted the corners, and white lights frosted angels and snowflake tunnels.

When he found her, he was almost brought to his knees by so many things: her earthy, shining beauty; her pure seductiveness; the guilt.

He'd spent more time at work today because, after David's convenient trip, Lucas had decided to approach some of the top executives and tell them straight out that he was going to be a more important part of TCO from now on. Since they knew he owned the majority of the stock, they heard him out. Lucas hadn't been asking for a rebellion against David or anything, but he had been laying groundwork in case the crap ever hit the fan.

As it just might if David decided to acknowledge Lucas's questions about what was happening with Tadmere.

He must've been staring at Alicia with such intensity that she felt it, because she met his gaze, matching it with the same heat.

His belly flip-flopped, arousing him.

As a notorious, very young heiress who was just coming of party age intercepted Alicia, his wife seemed to startle back to the moment. But after only a few minutes, she excused herself, leaving the room.

Gradually, the big-band music and the conversation filtered back to him. He laughed when he was supposed to laugh at his crowd's jokes, reacted when he was supposed to react, all while remaining on the fringes.

Where had she gone? And why did he miss her so much?

A short time later, he felt a pull on the back of his tux jacket. He turned around to find Alicia, who was smiling at the rest of the group. When Lucas saw the locker-room admiration in the other men's eyes, he bristled, slipping an arm around her waist.

"Mind if I borrow my husband?" she asked, all charm. A return to the hostess who'd enchanted him back at Refugio Salvo.

Before the group could answer, she'd pulled Lucas away, guiding him toward the door. "I checked in, and Gabriel is sound asleep. Magdelena's staying in the guest room tonight."

"How much longer do you want to hang out here?"

As she slipped her hand into his while they exited the ballroom, the hairs on his skin stood on end. God, one touch and he was a goner.

"I already thanked everyone who set up the event for

TCO," she said. "I told them you were coming down with something."

Well, since he hadn't been able to say much more than "boo" tonight during most conversations, he thought that might work. Going home sounded great to him. He'd been too consumed with his wife, because being away from her was a poison in his blood, killing him from the inside out.

She led him toward the lobby, and his body started echoing the distant rumba from the ballroom, deep and low.

One more day, one more day…

But when she pulled him into an elevator, suspicious hope clouded his vision. The car was thankfully empty, and, when she pressed a floor button, then wandered over to the opposite side to give him a shy glance, he began to give in to hope….

Her soft dress flowed around her, spotlighting the blush creeping up her face, emphasizing the sexy angel he'd come to need way too much.

"I couldn't stop watching you in there," she said, her blush deepening.

"Admiration from afar." Lucas tried to ignore the throb that was starting to beat in his groin. "Story of my life lately."

"I imagine you're not used to waiting for a woman. Especially your wife."

An inadvertent lump weighed in his throat, making his voice ragged. "Are you taking me to a room, Alicia?"

She touched that ever-present bracelet around

her wrist. Tonight, the charms were poking out of the pearls.

Slowly, she began to take both the pearls and the silver off, then secured them in her purse. Lifting her head, she looked him straight in the eye. There was a fire in her gaze, and it screwed into him like a column of heat.

"I didn't want to wait anymore," she said. "I mean—"

He was across the elevator in a flash, not caring if there were security cameras. Voraciously, he locked his mouth to hers, his fingers burying themselves in her hair with such tender roughness that pins hit the floor.

As her curls fell down to her shoulders, she answered him with such urgency that she seemed to blur into him, flame melding with flame. Before he knew it, his tux jacket was ripped open, his shirt jerked out of his pants.

The elevator doors parted, but it took him a moment to realize it. Still, Alicia must've been attuned to what was happening, because she dragged him into the hall, fumbling in her tiny evening bag.

"Key," she murmured.

Impatiently, he helped her find it and, between more kisses, they stumbled to a room she'd obviously booked when she'd disappeared from the event.

After the key had worked its magic, he pushed open the door, and it crashed against the wall. Lucas barely registered that it was a room, not a suite, but he didn't care. Hell, no. Alicia was all that mattered. His fantasies were coming true, his wife pulling him down to her for another long kiss as she dropped her bag to the floor.

He sipped at her, and she opened her mouth to him, allowing him to slip his tongue in. She was so warm, moist, tasting of a fruit cider they'd been serving downstairs.

His groin clutched, pounding with the blood roaring between his legs. He was getting so hard it pained him.

Slowing things down, he ran his tongue against hers, exploring in languorous time. It was seductive, delicious, but hardly appeasing his appetite.

It's actually happening, he thought, the realization knocking into him. He never thought he could feel this strongly about someone, but it wasn't as scary right now as he'd imagined. Not even close.

His arousal nudged against his fly, pushing him onward.

With a groan, he went deeper with his tongue, engaging hers in one long, sinuous stroke, then another. At the same time, he pressed into her, allowing her to feel his excitement. Her breasts were full, stimulating him to even greater heights as he imagined them bare in his palms.

Unable to hold back, he coaxed his hands around her, trying to locate a zipper. He didn't find one, discovering, instead, that there were intricate buttons down the front of the dress. He undid the first, then the next.

He heard her gasp, then pause, breathing against his mouth.

"Alicia?" he said, asking, needing.

After a pulse beat, he felt her nodding. "Yes. Yes."

He continued, heart in his throat. When he had the modest décolletage loosened, he saw that there was a bra built into it. With great care, he peeled the two sides back, revealing her full, naked breasts.

An emotion he couldn't name split him like a tree that'd been standing solid for years, only to be hit by lightning and transformed into new shapes that had opened themselves to the sky.

Her dusky nipples were tightened into buds, and greedily he ran a thumb over one, as if he'd discovered some rare gem.

"Why did you hide under so much clothing?" he asked.

"I…"

Wincing, she swallowed hard, leaning back her head.

He flowed with her momentum, guiding her toward the bed, laying her on it.

"You what, Alicia?"

She sighed, resting her head against a hand, glancing sidelong at him as he rubbed her nipple. She bucked slightly, then moved with his motions.

"Long story," she whispered tightly, closing her eyes. "But I…well, you know, I'm modest."

"Raised in a pious house. I know that. Are you afraid of making love with me?"

She bit her lip, and he had his answer…or, at least, part of it. He knew women who came from strict homes, but they'd gone against the grain, especially with him. In fact, it'd been as if a few of them had used Lucas Chandler to prove just how naughty they could be.

"It's not just sex," he said. "It won't be just sex with us, Alicia."

As the words echoed in his head, he wondered where the hell they'd come from. Even so, he knew with all his soul they were true. Lord, help him, they were true.

She opened her eyes, dark pools of mystery. "Lucas…"

"Yeah, angel?"

Almost sadly, she smiled at that. "Before we… I'm…" She blew out a breath, then watched him anxiously. "I'm not the angel you think I am. At least, not in that way."

Her meaning sank into him, and he stopped rubbing her breast for a second. "You're not a virgin."

"No." She said it as if she were crushed. "There was one time—"

He just about laughed, but that would've been a mistake. She was taking this seriously. Did she think he had some good girl/bad girl complex that would destroy him if he found out she wasn't pure? Well, he had called her his angel, but…he hadn't meant it that way. She was his angel because she'd saved him in so many ways.

"You really think that matters to me—a guy who's hardly pristine?"

She nodded, still gauging him.

Shaking his head, he stroked the underside of her breast. "You're twenty-three, and there aren't many women your age who haven't been with a man."

"So you don't care?"

"I care. I care about all your experiences and everything that's built you into the amazing woman you are. It wasn't your reputation that made me value you, Alicia, it's your…your soul, I suppose. Your actions. I'll take you any way you come."

Had he just said that? The playboy?

Yeah, he had, and he'd brought the smile of smiles to her. Now her eyes weren't dark with reluctance, they were beginning to shine with something else altogether. Invitation. Trust.

Leaving any guilt behind him—because how could he feel guilty about falling for her?—he cupped his hand under a breast, reveling in its curved weight. Primitive appreciation curdled in his belly, and he used his other hand to begin working her clothing off her, little by little.

As he bared her to him, he whispered gentle endearments, everything but the three words that really mattered. He couldn't love her, but he could honor and respect her in other ways. He could make this marriage a strong one, even if it'd started out for the wrong reasons.

He removed her shoes, then allowed the dress to fall to the carpet in a rustle of satin and chiffon, then tugged off her white cotton panties with both hands. Short of breath, he contained his crazed urges and sat back to worship her.

She was more beautiful than he could say, with her ample hips and curves, her smooth rosy-brown skin. He bent down to kiss her again, then used his lips to tattoo her from neck to collarbone.

Grasping his hair, she led him to her breasts, where he nipped and laved, taking her nipples into his mouth. He swirled his tongue over them, slow and deliberate, drawing them into even stiffer peaks.

"Oh…" she murmured, shifting beneath him.

By this time, his erection was howling for release, but he restrained himself. Alicia needed honey-slow seduction, and he was all for lingering inside of her when the time was right.

As she shifted in fevered demand, he took the next step, coasting a hand down, over her ribs, her stomach, to the thatch of dark hair between her legs. He eased a finger between her folds, hearing her moan.

"Are you happy, Alicia?" he asked.

"Almost," she ground out.

He laughed, feeling her getting primed for him. Pressing her nub, he drove her to squirm and cover her face with an arm.

Damn, he loved watching her like this, loved watching her in more sedate times when she was being a mother, too.

He loved…

Pushing the word away, he slipped a finger inside of her. She gasped loudly, lifting her hips, and he swirled, inside, out.

He was set to explode, but he'd wait. Dammit, he'd wait….

"Lucas…"

There it was, the final summons. Fumbling with his clothing, he nonetheless managed to get out of it and secure a condom from his wallet.

Soon, he was sheathed, poised over her to enter. "Ready…"

"*Yes.*"

Alicia wrapped a leg around him, pulling him down

to her. When he entered, there was momentary discomfort, but she set her teeth against it, grinding her hips against him with panting insistence. The bad girl was back, she thought, and Alicia had missed her. Heaven help her, she'd been so wrong about holding that girl back.

All but burning with a passion so frantic that she could barely restrain it, she welcomed her husband—her husband, not a disposable lover but a man who truly mattered—inside. She knew the difference only now, as he filled her with something more than the physical.

She was tight from her abstinence, but as she shifted back and forth, urging him to fit into her, the pain turned to pleasure, the shame blasted away by the good of what a married couple were meant to do.

While they moved together, her body riding the waves of his thrusts, every motion soothed her and stoked her.

Just the way...I am...

Values me... Wants me...

So right... So right...

The thoughts piled on one another until they seemed to reach the sky, trembling in a haphazard tower.

I love him, I love him....

The building blocks of her emotion quaked, rattling her bones, jittering against her skin, as Lucas drove harder into her, their bodies sticking together and sliding in exertion.

I love—

Without warning, a shot out of the darkness crashed

the tower. At the climax, she crumbled, tumbled, hit the ground with such force that she broke apart.

But she was so put together. So complete.

Soon he came to his own peak, and they held each other in their marriage bed.

In the quiet scatter of emotion, Alicia even thought she heard him say "I love you," but she was too over-wrought to know for sure.

"I love you, too," she whispered without restraint, the sentiment disappearing into the comforting blackness she saw when she closed her eyes. She nestled against him, flesh against flesh, her heart against his chest. "I love you, too."

Chapter Twelve

He'd told her he loved her.

Lucas sat in his office, his chair facing the window while he stared at a jagged skyline. It was Saturday, and TCO headquarters was subdued, populated by die-hard workaholics who didn't know the definition of what a weekend was.

Or by people who needed a place to sort things out.

His body still felt as alive as it had last night, fired with memories of caresses and sweat-slicked passion. After pressing against each other in the afterglow, he and Alicia had rested, stroking each other with quiet wonder, then gotten dressed in the midst of a new awareness.

Afterward, during the limo ride home, he'd found

himself unable to think of any light quips to chase away the silence. That's how he'd always handled sex in the past—a good time followed by the playboy's escape route: flattery that eased any disappointment his partner might have at his lack of commitment.

But he'd found himself much too committed last night, not wanting to let her go. Ever.

His confession—and hers—had reverberated around his skull.

Love. But how could he love a woman he was lying to?

When they'd gotten home, crossing the threshold hand in hand, their son had been asleep. As Lucas had kissed him in the night-light-dimmed room, it'd struck him: They were a real family. This wasn't an act, anymore, and he couldn't function under the weight of secrets, not if he really loved his wife and son, as he'd murmured in that one unguarded moment.

For the rest of the night, he'd tried to convince himself that his feelings were false, that they'd only been the product of finally getting what he wanted from Alicia's body. They made love once more, then again, but nothing changed.

Yet…he *couldn't* fall for her, he told himself over and over. He couldn't allow himself the luxury of it.

With the break of morning, when everything was more vulnerable in the light, Lucas panicked, cornered by his mistakes. Not knowing how to handle a kiss good-morning or even a breakfast with Gabe, he'd told his family that he needed to go into the office for a short time.

Now, at his desk, he held a hand to a pounding temple. How was he going to tell his wife what he'd done? Because, if he wanted to live with her, touch her, ever feel that he'd *earned* her, he needed to come clean.

But he knew exactly what the consequences would be—he'd *always* known. She would hate him and make his nightmares about becoming his own emotionally downtrodden father come true.

Dammit, he had no idea how to protect himself from what would inevitably happen. And to make things worse, there was a child's happiness and well-being at stake....

Behind Lucas's chair, someone cleared his throat. Lucas had forgotten Barnaby had come in, too, and they'd been having a conversation before Lucas's mind and body had collapsed into one big heap of muddled idiocy.

"Sorry about that," he said, swiveling back around until the view of his spartan office met him.

Barnaby sat in the middle of it all, a man dressed to the nines in a natty button-down shirt, tie and slacks. Surrounding him were Lucas's fledgling attempts at making his office more of a place he wanted to be: framed pictures of Alicia and Gabe by the Nativity scene, by the Christmas tree, on the couch lightly roughhousing one night before bedtime.

The photos both calmed Lucas and sent him into a mental upheaval once again.

"Glad I gave up Saturday morning to be here," Barnaby said, but he had a faintly ambitious glint in his eyes that told Lucas he was halfway kidding.

"Trying to sort a lot out." Lucas sighed, laying a hand on the reports Barnaby had set in front of him

about an hour ago, memos that his assistant had somehow intercepted. They confirmed that David had been
setting up meetings behind Lucas's back. "I hate to
think that my own brother would want to keep me in
the dark about a company I own, too, but…"

"But what more evidence do you need?"

"I'd like to hear him tell me to my face."

That's right—he wanted David to admit that he'd
had his eye on a woman like Alicia for Lucas all along.
And now Lucas wanted him to confess that he might
even be concerned about Lucas overstepping his Face
duties and stepping on David's Brain ones, too.

"What you need to do," Barnaby said, "is continue
impressing the other executives. The more you prove
that you're serious about this company, the more re-
ceptive they'll be. It's going to take a long time to erase
your reputation, but you should keep at it. Your work
with Refugio Salvo was an excellent start."

Lucas narrowed his gaze. Was Barnaby truly on his
side? Dumb question. Of course he was. If Lucas
gained power, he would be the assistant's golden ticket.
But he sensed something else—could it really be
respect?—as the other man picked up Lucas's favorite
picture from the desk, the one in front of the Christmas
tree.

"My family," Lucas said, pride flooding him, sur-
prising him with its strength.

Barnaby grinned at the photo. "In all honesty, I
thought you were a real fool before you got married,
Lucas. But you've turned it around. You really have."

He knew it was true. Alicia and Gabe had invaded

his soul. Maybe it was because he'd opened himself to changing after his father's stroke. Or maybe it was just because there was some kind of magic that one person saved for another one, and Alicia had been the woman to put a spell on him. Gabe, too.

But even in the light of this epiphany, a tug of fear still worked at Lucas.

What happens when the truth comes out? How will I cope if I don't protect myself?

From the doorway, a calm, low voice intruded.

"You're right, Barnaby," David said. "Lucas has really changed a lot."

He found his brother practically holding Ford Chandler up on one side as the older man used his silver-tipped cane to balance on the other. Their similarities wormed into Lucas: their dignified postures, their height and build. It occurred to him that David was on the fast track to becoming Ford Chandler, except, like the old Lucas, he'd taken care to avoid any emotional attachment to women. David Chandler would never emulate their dad in that respect.

"In the office on a weekend?" Ford asked, his eyes losing a little of their light. "This is serious."

At the veiled reference to Project Turning Over a New Leaf, Lucas's heart lurched—and not just because he was remembering Alicia. Clearly, Barnaby had known about this charade, but that didn't mean Lucas wanted him to hear this private talk.

David was giving Lucas's picture-riddled desk a measuring scan. His expression said what he was clearly thinking: *Yes. He's* very *serious.*

Setting down the Christmas-tree photo, Barnaby nodded at David and Ford. "I've got a lot of work waiting for me."

"And I've got a lot to talk about with my family," Lucas added. "Thank you, Barnaby. I really appreciate everything."

The assistant nodded again and headed for the exit as David led his dad farther inside. After the younger Chandler helped Ford to a couch, he closed the office door and made his way over to Lucas's desk, then picked up the photo Barnaby had deserted. After a second, he took it over to their dad, who smiled.

Lucas could hardly believe his father's receptiveness. Was Ford in the mood to put together another family, with a new wife? Or...

God, it was rough to consider that maybe, just maybe, the old man had changed after the stroke, too. That he'd started to make amends with his good-for-nothing son.

As if to prove it, his dad gave the picture back to David, his gaze misty. "I get to meet him tomorrow. My grandson."

Lucas could only nod, swamped by emotions he couldn't hold back. Respect. Here it was. So why didn't it feel better?

"You're really getting into the role," David said.

Heat crept up Lucas's skin, from his neck to his face. Part remembrance of last night, part anger at his brother. "We need to talk."

But David spoke up first. "Luke, here's a word of advice. Don't be carrying photos of that woman or the boy in your wallet or keeping them on your desk. All business. Just remember they're all business."

Are they? Lucas thought. *Have they ever been?*

On the couch, Ford didn't say anything. He just stared at the floor, leaning on his cane.

David was watching Lucas closely—too closely, as if he knew exactly what had happened at the ball last night. And maybe he did, with all the executives who were around to see how Lucas had lavished attention on his wife.

"Not that real emotion and passion for your charade is a bad thing," David said lightly even though his eyes were like granite. "The more genuine the act, the better. But I'd hate to see you break her heart with the truth."

"Bull." Lucas stood with such force that his chair hit the wall in back of him. "David, we've got something to hammer out here, so don't stir things up around Dad so you can avoid it. You flew out to L.A. on some useless trip just to make me stew. And did you bring Dad here to witness everything, hoping he'd see that I'm actually not fit to run the company, even in spite of all your 'support'?"

His brother didn't even try to deny it. He tapped the photo frame against his leg, the only sign of agitation. "You're *not* fit, Luke. Sure, you're great at a party and your marriage has done us a lot of good, so far, especially with Tadmere. But you're not executive material. Admit it."

From the couch, his father was watching with interest, as if seeing how Lucas would hold up under this onslaught. Lucas even thought he saw his dad urging him on with a subtle gaze, as if he didn't want to be disappointed by a human being, yet again, in the remaining time he had on earth.

Yet, how could Lucas not disappoint him? He'd already let *himself* down, and God knew how Alicia and Gabe would feel after they found out the truth. He hated who he was, hated the weakness in character that had allowed him to fall prey to David's orchestrations.

Protect yourself, his instincts yelled.

"I'm not the one who needs to do some admitting, David. Why didn't you tell me that Tadmere has television and radio stations across the border?"

David sent his dad a cocky glance. "Luke, if you'd possessed any interest in TCO, whatsoever, you'd have known. All of a sudden you're not trusting my business sense?"

"Not since I put two and two together. Tadmere and their Mexican interests. Our need to get in good with their customers. Your proposal to have me court not just a good woman but one whose ethnicity could be used to sway the demographics."

"Come on, Luke, would you have said no to a relationship with her even if you'd known what all of the plan entailed? I just didn't involve you in the more unsavory details because I didn't think you needed them to function as the Face. Besides—" he raised an eyebrow "—you're the one who went and put a family together."

Stung, Lucas thought about how much he'd just wanted to please his father with this new reputation. How he would've done anything—*had* done anything.

Knowing that David had planned to exploit Alicia's ethnicity wouldn't have held him back because he'd wanted to be a "better man" too damned badly.

He'd just gone about it all wrong.

He glanced at his dad, finding that the old man looked more exhausted than ever. Was he hoping Lucas had some kind of heart, after all?

How could Lucas finally please him, once and for all?

Anger riding his words, he decided that maybe the truth should start here, in front of his father. "There's a difference in what we perceived a relationship with Alicia to be, David. She was…" His heart swelled. "I really wanted to be with her, just because of who she was, not because she was a statistic or political ploy. I needed her and Gabe's goodness in my life. Marriage was the excuse that finally allowed me to admit that I was missing something only she and my son could give me."

Sapped by the admission, Lucas planted his hands on the desk, almost afraid to look at his father. But he did. Dammit, if he was any kind of man, he could face the most influential person in his life—the dad who'd been such a cold role model, the paternal figure who held such inexplicable power over Lucas.

He found the old man's eyes watery with a pain he seemed to be reliving before Lucas's very gaze. His wives. Maybe he was recalling each one of his own heartbreaks, each vow he'd made to never fall into a woman's trap again.

Maybe he didn't want Lucas to fall into it, either. Or was there more to it? Was this a test?

Probably. Lucas was too used to the father who'd been so stony to him while growing up. Maybe Ford Chandler wanted to see if his son was tough enough to run a corporation and that's why he wasn't explaining anything.

Did he want to discover if Lucas would be destroyed by a woman, too? Or did he just want his son to be happy now?

"Luke," David said, looking as if he felt sorry for his brother. "Think about what you're saying. Do you really believe you're the type of man who can make Alicia happy beyond money? Seriously?"

It was as if all his doubts had been given a voice.

His defense mechanisms revved up again, because when Alicia found out what he'd done, he would end up just like the old man. Crushed and wounded, sidelined by a frail body and heart.

Maybe you just need to tell her everything before you fall even further for her, his defenses screamed. *Maybe David's right, and you should just push her away before she finds out herself how useless you are.*

"Anyway," David added, looking at the Christmas-tree picture once more, then discarding it on the desk, facing it away from him, "you'll be happy to know that our plan at least worked. Tadmere's executives loved Alicia and they had a lot to do with persuading the big bosses to trust us. It seems that they think you chose well when it came to a wife and that all the rumors about you might've been…inflated. So early this morning, over breakfast, the Tadmere siblings signed the company over to us."

David seemed to want to high-five him or something, but there was no celebration in Lucas. Just a dull, empty space that had opened up, swallowing all the hope and love he thought he'd had for Alicia and Gabe.

It wasn't real. It was all just a plan that had worked out for the betterment of TCO.

Over on the couch, Ford Chandler sighed, speechless.

And, behind the barricade of his desk, Lucas glanced at the Christmas-tree picture of him, Alicia and Gabe, all huddled in a laughing group and smiling at the camera without any show or pretense.

She was going to turn him away when she found out about this marriage.

She was going to surprise him.

Alicia couldn't just sit at home, waiting for her husband to get back. Not when she was obsessed with replaying every single touch and kiss, her body urging her to be with him again, to seek out more, more, more.

So she'd put together a basic snack in a wicker basket: sliced smoked Gouda cheese with dainty crackers, apples and oranges, sparkling mineral water, freshly baked chocolate-chip cookies. Though she knew that he would, no doubt, attend some expense-account, high-class restaurant for a noontime meal, her efforts were an excuse to go to him, to extend their afterglow.

So this was what love felt like, she thought, kissing Gabriel goodbye as he built a skyscraper out of lettered wooden blocks with Magdelena's help. She promised she would be home in a couple of hours—and she meant it, knowing she would miss Gabriel after a short time.

But this was her honeymoon, and she needed to be alone with her husband.

She also needed to finally tell him everything that had been haunting her. The truth about who she really was, the ugliness about how she'd been conceived. Now, more than any other time, she knew Lucas would accept her, warts and all. Hadn't he said as much last night?

I'll take you any way you come, he'd told her, and she'd believed it. The soulful way he'd made love to her had only confirmed that, too, creating a confidence she'd never possessed before meeting him. She had nothing to be afraid of.

On the way over in the town car, she called ahead. He wasn't answering his cell, so she tried his work number. She was forwarded to his assistant, Barnaby, who was also working on a Saturday. Smiling at Lucas's ambition to be a bigger part of the company, she thought that, as long as he still spent all that time with her and Gabriel, she wouldn't complain.

Barnaby arranged for her to be let in, and a fawning security guard escorted her to the fortieth floor. The assistant greeted her at the elevators.

"Mrs. Chandler, it's wonderful to finally meet you."

She was so anxious to get to Lucas that she probably sounded rude when she refused his escort and asked how to get to her husband's office by herself, instead.

But Barnaby seemed to understand as he gave her directions.

"Thank you so much." She reached into the basket, gave him some cookies. "Hope you get to go home soon."

She waved farewell as she walked toward her husband's office.

It wasn't hard to find, with his name embossed in gold plating on the door. She knew Barnaby had told him to expect her, so she wasn't surprised to discover him alone at his desk.

What she hadn't expected was his dark gaze.

"Hi," she said hesitantly, wondering if she'd interrupted something important with her snacktime whim.

Yet, when he smiled at her, his eyes lighting up just an instant before the joy switched off again, she wasn't so sure that he hadn't been waiting just for this moment, when he could talk to her.

Was something wrong?

He helped her put the basket on the desk, their fingers brushing and sending flares up her skin. He grinned again, flashing dimples, and she thought maybe she'd been imagining everything.

"I've missed you," he said, leaning over and kissing her.

As their lips fused, she sank into the searing delights of last night's lovemaking, her body reliving the ecstasy.

"Me, too," she said against his lips. "I couldn't stay away."

Kissing her again, he gathered her against him, holding her so tightly she thought she might break apart if he hadn't been the glue that held her together.

He pulled her onto the desk until she was sitting.

Files shifted over the top of the wood, but he didn't mind. She was the most important thing on his to-do list, obviously, and that brought back her self-esteem, full-roar.

Releasing him, she reached into the basket and began to parcel out the food. "Getting lots done?"

He paused, turned away from her to snatch an apple. He stared at it, his gaze going hard again. "Too much. I'd love to forget about all of it."

With force, he bit into the fruit. Heart aching for him to touch her again, she caressed his arm. She could make him forget anything, could make him think that she was the only person who existed. She was positive of that.

"I want to tell you something that's been bugging me," she blurted, a little shocked that it'd just come out like this. But she'd been talking herself into spilling everything all the way over here and she didn't want to wait, anymore.

For a second, he seemed reluctant to hear what she had to say, so she rushed to explain. "It's not about you, believe me. In fact, last night, everything you said, what you made me feel… I want you to know who I am before we go on. You deserve to know, wife to husband. I don't want there to be anything between us, anymore."

Slowly, he set down the apple.

She had to get it all out before he looked any more worried. She hated making him uncomfortable like this.

Taking a breath, a twinge of panic almost made her stop before she'd started. This private knowledge had marked her so deeply, so awfully, that letting it out was almost like opening a Pandora's box.

But it was the right thing to do. No secrets. Lucas was going to love her any way she came.

Going for it, she forced the story into the open, telling him about her grandfather's deathbed confession—her papa's prostitution, the one-night stand that had turned into a pregnancy, the abandonment.

All the while, Lucas never seemed judgmental. In fact, he seemed shattered in some heartbreakingly silent way. Still, he kept his distance while she spoke.

Heart racing, she ended the story. "I tried to find them, both my mom and dad, but I kept running into dead ends."

"That's why you sold your home and went to Mexico."

"Yes." She plucked at the skirt of her suit. "It's almost like I was led down there, to find Gabriel. To find you."

He fixed his gaze on the floor.

A snap of doubt nagged at her. "I didn't want you to regret having a marriage that turned out to be a lot different than what you first thought it would be."

It was as if she'd slapped him with that last statement.

In a terrible instant, her fears crashed over her. Had she been wrong? Was he disgusted by her now that he realized he was committed to someone with a background that would dirty his new lease on life? Was he afraid of the bad press she'd bring now?

The returning shame throttled her even before she could shield herself with the reminder of everything he'd told her about accepting her, valuing her.

"Marriage," he repeated, closing his eyes and running a hand through his hair. "Alicia, I…" He shook his head. "Dammit, you don't have anything to be ashamed of. Not at all."

Of course Lucas didn't think any less of her because of this story. Alicia wasn't responsible for the sins of her father, even if she'd been raised to believe the opposite. But that wasn't the reason he was ripped up.

No, his self-disgust had hit him with a vengeance, barring him from even glancing at her. Lies, all his lies, when she was so intent on the truth… He didn't deserve even a look, a touch—nothing from this woman. And, just as David had said, Lucas knew he would never deserve her.

He hadn't even earned the privilege of being a father to Gabe, who needed to grow up knowing the value of truth.

God, his son. Lucas's heart cracked.

Instinct urged him to protect himself. To keep his world together before she exercised her power to tear it apart by rejecting *him*.

Before he could even think, he moved to the other side of the desk, removing himself from the temptation of her skin, her perfume, memories of the beautiful life they could've had. "I've done something that…"

This was it, but he couldn't go on, not when he wanted to hold on to what he'd found in Alicia and Gabe so damn badly.

At first, she just smiled at him, so innocently that it slayed him. "What have you done besides make me and Gabriel happy, Lucas?"

But as he stood in silence, she seemed to catch on

to the seriousness of what he was about to tell her. One of her hands grabbed at the edge of his desk.

"Lucas, what're you talking about?"

You don't deserve her, instinct screamed. *You never will, so let her go before this goes any further.*

"Our marriage—" his voice was tight in his throat "—it's a sham."

Chapter Thirteen

Lucas's announcement still bounced off the walls, punching Alicia with hollow ripples of sound that invaded her but didn't hurt. No, they didn't hurt just yet, even though they should have.

He was saying he really *didn't* love her, right? That he wasn't accepting her, after all?

As she endured the mental pummeling, her gaze locked onto the pictures on his desk, as if she needed to cling to some kind of friendly anchor.

Christmas trees, Nativity scenes, Gabriel clowning in front of the camera, Alicia and Lucas with their arms around each other, their skin touching and nearly fusing with the warmth that always connected them…

Jokes, Alicia thought, as the pictures warped in the hot tears flooding her eyes. *Tragic jokes caught on film.*

Across the desk, she was aware of how Lucas was waiting for her to react, his body taut.

The body she'd rubbed up against last night, the body that had joined hers in a reverent, personal matrimony.

Sham... It didn't make any sense. He'd said he loved her. He'd even shown her that. And she'd welcomed the love as if it'd been a part of her that had finally come home.

"I—" she shook her head "—I don't understand."

"You should know the truth." He'd become so cold, so unlike the man she'd come to cherish.

As her gaze locked back onto him, the room blurred even more, and not only because of the tears. Nothing was clear.

But then a teardrop fell from one eye and she caught a bleary half view of him. Unlike the normally light-hearted man who operated under such charm and stature, Lucas looked beaten, his shoulders hunched, his face mapped with devastation. He was a mirror of the pain that was just beginning to scald her as the truth of his statement seeped into her.

"I married you specifically to clean up my public image and to help TCO acquire Tadmere," he said, voice rigid, agonized.

Hadn't he already decided to redo his life when he'd met her? And hadn't their marriage just happened, without any plans, whatsoever? It almost sounded as if she'd been part of some clinical scheme....

He was watching Alicia as if asking for her to yell at him, to wound him. But she was too numb.

It must've been the shock that made her say, "Are you telling me this because you think I'm not good enough for you now?"

"No. That's…God, that's not it, at all, Alicia."

Nonetheless, the deeply engraved fear ached. Shrinking into herself, she instinctively buried her face in her hands. Suddenly, her fancy new clothing felt like a hard shell that hung off her with an alien weight; she longed for her old clothes, her old life.

Maybe the agony would disappear if she went far enough into that shell.

"Alicia."

She heard him move toward her, but she angled her body away, the motion edged with an anger she was only now admitting.

"I don't blame you for hating me." His voice was ravaged. "I'm sorry. I did it because Tadmere wouldn't sell unless I polished up my act."

He'd done it for his dad, too, she thought. For his dad, not for her or Gabriel.

Ire was eating her up, gnawing its way through her uncomfortable designer suit. She raised her face from her hands, realizing her fingers were damp.

"So there it is," she said, her stomach quivering from repressed rage. But if there was one thing she'd learned from loving this man it was that holding back was ridiculous. She'd done it too long because of her parents and she'd realized last night that it'd been a mistake.

Now she wasn't going to restrain anything.

"Your poor inner playboy made you do it?" she said, facing him.

He was obviously struggling for control. "I won't make excuses."

"Then what other reason could there be, Lucas?"

Before the question was even out of her mouth, it all hit her, each piece clicking into place. How he'd seduced her with promises of family when he knew damn well she wanted it more than anything. How he'd accelerated their courtship by telling her he wouldn't be around for long and that they should live for the moment. How she'd heard David mention demographics on the phone. How Lucas had been concerned by Tadmere's ownership of Mexican companies. How Lucas had taken a Latina wife just as TCO was getting more desperate to buy Tadmere, which owned Mexican outlets.

"There's more to it, too," he said as she slipped off the desk and almost stumbled toward the windows, away from him. "Besides polishing my life for public consumption with a storybook relationship, it was only later I found out that Tadmere had holdings across the border. Getting together with you was a good way to court Tadmere's executives, as well as the people who'd be listening to and watching the stations down there."

"I was good PR. You chose me because of my ethnicity."

"No."

She heard the rustle of his clothing as he came nearer, but the sound only ratcheted up her anger.

"Stay—" she turned to him and held up a hand; it trembled "—away." Shaking her head, she held back a new attack of tears.

For a fleeting moment, he went from ice-cold to thawed, one hand stretched out to her in supplication. Even so, she couldn't reconcile what she was hearing with the family they'd become, the love they'd just started to share.

With his betrayal.

It occurred to her that this arrangement was the reason he hadn't forced the honeymoon issue, but she was hardly grateful. Allowing her to decide when the time was right was the least he should have done.

Even if the part of her that still loved him gave him credit for it.

"So you didn't choose me because of my background when that's what TCO needed to secure Tadmere?" she asked.

"I didn't deceive you about that part, Alicia. I really didn't know about the Mexican businesses." That muscle in his jaw flinched and he fisted his hands by his sides, as if arming himself. "David's the one who suggested a relationship, but I wanted the marriage and adoption. *I* did. He only planted the idea in my head after he saw the obvious attraction between us."

"Attraction." Such a casual way to describe what she thought they'd had.

But there was something much more important at stake here. Gabriel. Oh, Gabriel.

"The worst thing about this," she said, on the cusp of tears again, "is Gabriel. That child loves you, Lucas, and you've set him up to be abandoned again. Didn't you think about that?"

"I did, over and over again." Unclenching his fists

at the mention of Gabriel, Lucas seemed to succumb to the self-loathing she'd seen so many times, the destructive pattern she'd wanted to save him from. "I thought about what I was doing to the both of you every day. But in that moment I proposed to you, I knew I could give him a good home. And I thought I could make you happy. Believe that, at least. I really thought I could."

At his forced tone, something yanked at the core of her, yet she ignored it. She had to or else she'd be twice the idiot she was now. Lord, help her, she wasn't about to suffer because of someone else's sins again.

She wouldn't waste one more precious second doing that.

"So what do you want?" she asked. "Am I supposed to pretend this is okay? That a trip to Rockefeller Center or a shopping spree will get things back to normal?" Back to the happiness she'd experienced for such a short, wonderful time?

"I don't expect you to forget. But..." He stiffened again, then turned around, revealing an icy gaze that was much too close to David's. Yet, there was something below that frosty glance...almost as if there was a plea in the depths of color, a cry to make him stop. "I can make this marriage worth your while, Alicia. Gabe has a home and we can keep it that way. And you've got the money for your charities, you've got a family. Maybe I can't give you more than that—"

It was as if she'd been slammed off the edge of the earth.

Cheap. *Dios,* was she so cheap that he thought she could be bought off?

He really didn't value her. She'd been wrong. So, so wrong.

"You're making me feel like I'm my father," she said, hardly able to talk with the emotional grit in her throat. "You make me feel as if I can be had for money. I never thought you'd be the one to do that to me."

At her pain, he seemed to crumble, his gaze turning sorrowful, his hand rising again as if begging her.

Seeing this strong man completely defeated almost undid her. Her impulsive, love-stricken side wanted to run to him, to find a way to work this out. Because, in a way, he was right—why throw away what they had? Why take away Gabriel's family? The family she'd been praying for?

Yet, she couldn't forget this. He'd taken advantage of the poor little girl he thought she was, exploited her need for acceptance.

"I won't be your pawn," she whispered.

He jerked as if impaled, just as she'd been earlier, but she took no satisfaction from it. Yet, she wouldn't allow herself to sympathize with him.

Not anymore, she thought. Not after this.

Dear God, why couldn't she just find someone to love her? Her parents, now Lucas... What was wrong with her that they all treated her so badly?

And to think she'd almost had her family. So close. So, so close.

She grabbed at her jacket, pulled at it to keep her emotions in check, to keep herself in that shell, secure.

"Odd," she said softly, "I almost believed that there's dignity in love, but I can't imagine there is now." Her chest pulled itself apart with sadness as she prepared to go. "I almost left the shame behind, but this brings it to a new level."

As Lucas watched her leave, a tortured groan escaped him. He moved toward her retreating form but held himself back, just as he'd been holding back all the real truths in an attempt to defend himself from the rejection he knew was coming.

He did love her, so much. And now that she was turning her back on him, he couldn't control it anymore.

But hadn't he been right about the outcome? All his worst fears had come true because now she was abandoning him. But he deserved her scorn, deserved every harsh truth she could dish out.

"I'd give anything for you to forgive me," he said as he went to the door, his shields wearing down. "I don't want you to hurt, Alicia. I'd take all your pain on me if I could."

In the hallway, when she glanced back at him with those watery eyes, he thought that maybe, just maybe, she believed him. But then her doubt returned, barring her from his best intentions.

Couldn't she believe in him enough to think that maybe he could change someday if she stayed?

No, God no, he thought. He'd destroyed her ability to trust him, and that left him with next to nothing.

In fact, he *was* nothing because, without her, he was just a tycoon playboy who had no emotions or heart. An empty good-time guy who wasn't capable of anything more.

It was true. Now that she was leaving him, he realized that living with her and taking the risk of getting decimated by love was so much better than coming home to an empty place.

He needed her forgiveness. Needed her and Gabe. He didn't want to live without them, even if it meant he would be as ruined as his father was now.

She was shaking her head, fending off his plea for a second chance. "Maybe I can forgive you, but I can't forget, Lucas. I can't forget how I was just a thing to you."

"You aren't. Listen to me, Alicia, you're…" *Say it.* "You're my world." His ears rang with the emotional outburst, but he meant it. Meant it with all of his soul. "You and Gabe."

With a stifled sob, she rushed down the hall.

"Alicia, don't go! Don't hide. Don't run away from this like you did when you sheltered yourself in Mexico, in the orphanage, under those strict clothes and vows."

Whipping around, she revealed a face streaked with the red trails of tears. "I'm still that woman, plain and simple! And thinking I'm anything that'll fit into this fake life of yours is just another lie!"

She shot him a look that he interpreted as, *And thinking you're anything more than a playboy is a lie, too.*

Or maybe that was his conscience giving him that final kick in the gut.

Whatever it was, he watched her run down the rest of the hallway, then disappear around the corner, out of his sight.

Losing the last of his hope and strength, he slumped against the wall, allowing it to hold him up.

Gone, he thought. *The best thing that's ever happened to you is gone, and you're the reason she left.*

But that was no huge surprise, because wasn't that the way of things? His father had always reminded him that women leave. He'd seen it with stepmother after stepmother.

And Lucas's woman—the wife he'd fallen head over heels for—was leaving, too, because he was too weak to hold on to her.

But, God, he loved her more than anything, loved Gabe more than he could've ever imagined.

The thought held him up, even without the wall, as he trained his gaze down the hallway, his mind furiously scrambling for ways to keep his family from falling apart.

At first, Alicia had cried so much that the tears had become meaningless. On the way back to the penthouse in the town car, on the trip up in the elevator, in the taxi she had summoned once she had quickly packed enough clothing and toys to comfort Gabriel as she blindly searched for direction…

Now, two weeks later, as she watched her son playing with a Slinky on the withered carpet of the motel room she could barely afford with her own money, Alicia was done with tears. They hadn't helped her to decide where to go from here or how to drive the love she had for Lucas out of her heart.

He had called on her cell phone over and over again, asking her to meet with him. But she hadn't returned any of his messages, even if his voice was ragged with remorse.

"I'll do anything to make this up to you, Alicia," he'd said from the first phone call on. "Please, just believe that."

Every day, every hour, every *minute*, Lucas's heartfelt confession at the office played over and over in her head, as if it'd been recorded on a loop and she'd been strapped to a chair and sentenced to listen to it for hours on end.

You're my world. You and Gabe...

But what about love? Had she just imagined hearing it that night at the Christmas fund-raiser? Why wasn't he mentioning the one thing that just might make her reconsider?

He'd proposed that they keep their business marriage together, but he hadn't said he loved her. That told her everything.

On the floor, Gabriel dropped the Slinky, his lower lip wobbling as he turned to her.

He didn't need to say anything, because Alicia knew that face. The big, sad brown eyes filled with questions she hadn't been able to answer.

Why aren't we living with Daddy? You let me see him every night, Mama, but you never stay for dinner with us. Why, why, WHY?

"Are you ready to go to Daddy's now?" she asked, throat raw. It'd be cruel to keep her son away from Lucas, so she'd worked out temporary visitation via Magdelena. The boy loved his adopted dad beyond measure, and she knew Lucas felt the same way about his new son. But that didn't make coming to any decisions easier.

Gabriel brightened up for a moment, clearly joyful at the prospect of visiting with Lucas. Alicia had offered up the lame excuse that Daddy and Mama were on a "vacation" from each other, because it was the only thing she could think to tell him. The truth would hurt Gabriel beyond imagination.

Sheltering him from the truth was the only option she could come up with right now.

As she led her son to a waiting taxi she'd reserved for every night at this hour—dinnertime with Daddy— she once again tried to think of a better story for Gabriel, something with a happier ending. She was always going to be his mother, no matter how much she had to scrimp and save to stay in New York so he could keep visiting Lucas. But how would her so-called husband fit into their future? She had no idea, but it was obvious *she* wouldn't be able to live with him anymore.

Right? Wasn't it obvious?

You're my world. You and Gabe...

Alicia's chest caved into itself while the taxi traveled from Jamaica and into Manhattan. Soon they were inching along Fifth Avenue, the sidewalk traffic visible from the tinted windows. Gabriel merely stared outside from the height of his car seat, face devoid of its usual glow.

Not for the first time, guilt hit her full force. How could she deprive her child of Lucas's genuine affection? Of the privilege Gabriel would enjoy if she could only allow herself to take the first step and give Lucas the chance to make it up to her as he wished to?

And how can you deprive yourself of the man you love?

Gripping the material of her modest skirt, Alicia

pushed away her fear and watched the view, too. All those people buzzing around, shopping for gifts three days before Christmas, enjoying the sights of the city, bundled against the twilight chill. She wished she could be one of them, with Christmas on her mind and "Jingle Bells" playing through her head instead of all her regrets and doubts.

Two weeks ago, before she'd known the truth, everything had seemed so beautiful. She'd been so ecstatic, just like life with her grandparents before her *abuelo* had told her about the taint of her birth. Ignorance had, indeed, been bliss.

But then the poison apple of wisdom had fallen into her hands and Eden had been taken away from her.

Anger reemerged, but it wasn't necessarily at Lucas now—it was at circumstance.

Why was she allowing something other than herself to control what she really wanted? A family. A life full of nights with the Lucas she'd fallen in love with.

Why was she bowing to outside forces and surrendering her happiness to them again? *Why?*

The more she dwelled on it, the more rebellious she became. Oddly enough, she knew that Lucas still valued her. His courtship had proven that over and over; either that or he'd been a very good actor. But she didn't buy that at all—she knew deep down he had felt something for her.

Love?

She recalled that day in the office, when he'd finally laid his emotions at her feet before she'd run away from him. Would a man like him—one who feared abandonment himself—have continued calling her, begging her to listen to him unless he really did love her? Why wasn't he repeating it again and again on the phone then?

That was the only thing holding her back. If she could just hear him say it…

Twenty minutes later, Alicia and Gabriel stepped into the penthouse elevator at the Boudin, a familiar, painful experience. The marbled elegance that had once felt so alien now seemed like an abandoned part of home, because that's where it had once led.

Home, with the man she still loved, even after everything.

At the end of the ride—Gabriel hadn't even enjoyed it as he usually did, she noted with sinking disappointment—they came to the lobby.

"Daddy's not home yet," Alicia said. She'd been careful in arranging to drop her son off with Magdelena before Lucas was scheduled to leave the office in a half hour. "But he'll be here soon."

"Mama come for food?" Gabriel said as Alicia rang the doorbell. Hope kindled in his dark gaze.

"Not tonight." She smoothed back the hair from his face.

"Why no?"

Again blank spaces served as answers.

Why? Why won't you give Lucas a chance to redeem himself? Didn't you once believe he was capable of becoming that good person he wished to be?

As she flailed for a decent response, the door eased open.

Revealing the one person she'd been trying so hard to avoid.

At the sight of him, she couldn't take in oxygen. Dizziness swept over her, her belly clenching with such force that she almost weakened, throwing herself into his arms. She'd been so afraid this would happen if they came face-to-face.

Yet, all she wanted to do was be near him, against him.

His lips parted as if to say something, but he didn't speak. No, his reddened, desperate gaze said it all.

His devastation, still fresh after all these days, hammered at her. So did his appearance. It looked as if every hour had taken a swing at him, connecting with bruising mental force that had beaten the life out of him.

Sorrow tightened the area behind her eyes. *Lucas.*

"Daddy!" Gabriel yipped, throwing himself into Lucas's arms.

Tearing his gaze away from Alicia, her husband broke into an anguished smile, grabbed on to his son as if his life depended on it.

"It's been just one day and I missed you," he said into the boy's hair. "I've missed you so much."

"Me, too!" Gabriel had latched his arms around Lucas's neck and wasn't letting go.

Before Alicia could break down, she took a step backward. "I'll see you in a few hours, Gab—"

"No, wait, Alicia," Lucas said. "Wait?"

Whispering into his son's ear, Lucas let the child go. Gabriel yelped, taking off into the penthouse. As if not wanting to break the connection, Lucas watched the boy disappear.

"I've been waiting to see you, too," he said softly. "Come in?"

She caught a whiff of Italian food. The scent broke one of the threads holding her together, leaving her dangling. But she didn't look at him. She couldn't, not if she wanted to keep herself from getting her heart thrashed to pieces again....

"I have to go."

"Don't." He stepped over the threshold. "I made sure I'd be here to see you tonight. Enough is enough. Please stay here, listen to me." His shoulders lost some of their heft. "I want you to see that I really have changed because of you and Gabe, even though I know you won't forgive me. I can't blame you for that, but I want to try."

As Lucas waited for her answer, he swallowed hard. Honoring her requests for maintaining distance had gotten to him. He hadn't wanted to disrespect her by hunting her down at her motel room, didn't want to force her to take money to maintain her separate residence, either. He'd known she wouldn't accept anything from him, but he'd done everything he could, anyway—except tell her that he loved her over the phone. It wasn't something to be said over an impersonal distance. He'd been waiting weeks to do it in person, knowing the words would sound cheap unless she could *see* just how much he meant it.

Only problem was, she'd be able to see how much of a disaster he'd become since she'd left him.

Alicia was eyeing him as if he were going to reach into her chest and yank out her heart—but he'd already accomplished that. Now all that was left to do was return it and hope that she would give it to him again with as much love as he felt for her.

"Stay," he said, the word raspy.

She looked like she wanted to enter so badly, yet she waited a beat, as if expecting him to say more.

And he would, if she would just come into their home.

Inside, he'd set up an I-love-you dinner that would show her just how much he meant it—everything from hundreds of roses to a recreation of their first meal together from Bella Sofia. But he'd made *this* meal himself, with a little help from Magdelena. He wanted everything to come from his heart, his soul.

He wanted her to know, without a doubt, that she meant everything to him.

He hesitated, suddenly unsure of himself, even though he saw how she felt clearly, agonizingly.

What if she's just not going to give you another chance? he thought, chest constricting. *What if she's beyond grand gestures—*

But then Gabriel ran into the foyer, and Lucas tore his gaze away from Alicia's for only a moment. How could he resist with his son?

"Rose!" the little boy said, holding up a thornless flower to his daddy, as if in sweet offering.

But all he saw were the elevator doors smacking closed.

She was gone.

Then realization crashed in on him. *You should've told her how much you love her right away, dammit. You didn't need fireworks to give her what she wanted.*

He bent down to give Gabriel a fierce hug, then whispered a promise in the boy's ear.

"I'll be right back, okay?" He strode out the door to go after Gabriel's mommy.

The wife he wasn't going to lose again.

Alicia leaned her forehead against the wall of the elevator car, eyes closed.

She'd given Lucas the chance to tell her, but he hadn't said it. The only words she'd wanted to hear, and he hadn't been able to come out with them.

I. Love. You.

That was it. Simple and pure. And she'd thought she'd read the sentiment in his eyes, but…

She opened her eyes as the doors opened, allowing her to walk into the Boudin's lobby and straight to the waiting taxi that would take her back to the motel.

She entered the taxi, ensconced in its heat, but the warmth didn't go any deeper as the car pulled into the street. No, all that remained within her was a stillness, the feeling of a house that'd been emptied of its furniture and life.

She'd only wanted to hear an *I Love You*….

The taxi driver's low voice startled her.

"New York idiots," he said, glancing at his side-view mirror. "A moron is running up through the traffic, ma'am. But do not worry—our doors are locked, so you are safe from him, okay?"

Before she could react, there was a pounding at her window. She jerked away from it, hand to her throat.

As her eyesight adjusted, she saw Lucas, face flushed, eyes wild as he held up his hands in a plea.

"I love you, Alicia!" he yelled.

Her body flamed. *I love you,* he'd said, truth in his steady gaze. His admission bounced through her mind like the echoes of a triumphant chorus.

And he'd come after her. *Her.* His wife.

Something like a laugh—or maybe a sob of relief—shook her. "I…" The words had caught in her throat, so she cleared it, digging into her coat pocket and offering a fistful of money—how much, she didn't know—to the driver.

"Please unlock the door. My ride's done."

"Ma'am?" the cabbie asked.

"Please."

She heard the driver do as she asked. Right away, Lucas pulled it open, and a blast of cold air enveloped her.

"I saw you take off in this cab and ran you down," he said, grabbing her hands and taking her out of the taxi. "I'm not letting you get away this time. I love you. I mean that and I'll say it a million times to get you to believe it."

Horns blared at them, imitating the volume of her growing joy as it consumed her. While she caught her breath, Lucas held up a hand at the waiting vehicles, then pulled her to the sidewalk, where people dodged them.

Alicia barely felt the brush of their coats against her body. All she knew was that Lucas really wasn't going to surrender her without a fight.

That he *loved* her.

Holding her hands tightly, Lucas was dressed only in his cotton shirt, his cheeks flushed with cold.

But he didn't seem to mind that. "I fell for you the instant I saw you. And Gabe...I saw myself in him and I knew right away I couldn't live without him, either. But I wasn't honest with you about why I asked you to be my family. I couldn't be."

"Lucas—"

"Please just hear me out, because I'm never holding anything back again. It took me a long time to come to terms with how I felt because I thought opening myself up to you would make me weaker, just like my dad." He raised her hands to his chest, where she could feel his heart pounding. "But, all along, something was telling me it would be okay and I gave in, convincing myself that I was marrying you for business and never realizing the truth—that I wanted you more than any woman I've ever met. That I wanted to protect Gabe and keep him from all the disappointments I saw in his future."

Tears had started to slip from her eyes, coating her face. He reached out dry them.

"I'm willing to endure whatever punishment you have in store for me," he said. "I just want to go home with you. I want to hold on to all the good that came out of a bad situation. Please, Alicia."

Her breath hitched on a sob and she couldn't say anything.

"Okay. You still think our marriage can't be real." His tone was jagged, desperate. "Then I'm going to take care of that."

Right in the middle of the sidewalk he fell to his

knees, holding her hand between his again, almost as if he were in prayer. His violet eyes locked onto hers and in them Alicia could see a universe of love. It rocked her until her knees shook, threatening to take her down.

Voice raised, he said, "Alicia Sanchez Chandler, marry me again. I love you more than any man could ever love a woman. I'll love you until we're both old and our children need to wheel us around. I love you with all my heart."

Some people on the sidewalk had stopped to stare. There were even some mutters of "Lucas Chandler?"

Yet, he was oblivious, watching her with unadulterated hope, his emotions bare.

He loved her. He'd said it, not in the dark of night but in broad daylight in front of everyone. It was real. Pure and real, no matter what her worst fears told her.

How could she live without this man? How could she not give him another chance?

At her hesitation, a woman from the crowd said, "Girl, you'd better say yes before *I* do."

"Aren't they already married?" said another.

Alicia ignored them. Lucas Chandler was hers. She'd known it right from the start. She couldn't let him get away, couldn't miss this opportunity for happiness, even if they would both have to work for it.

Emotion overrode fear, her answer bursting out from the bottom of her soul.

"Yes," she whispered. "Yes, I'll be your wife."

As the growing crowd broke into "aws" and applause, Lucas jumped up and scooped her into his arms, hugging her to him until she almost lost her breath.

Amidst the clapping, he whispered in her ear, "I

know we have a lot to talk about, but I wanted to make you see that I'm serious. That this isn't any secret plan. Not anymore."

"I know. I love you, too. I always have."

She kissed him, the people around them whooping and cheering them on. Their voices merged into a chorus, a holiday carol of celebration and togetherness, a hymn of perpetual love.

When he set her on her feet, looking into her eyes and cupping her face in his hands, she eased off her coat, shedding at least part of her shell. She slipped it around him, just as he'd done for her that first day they'd met, then again on the penthouse terrace when she'd felt so out of sorts and he'd known just what she needed.

Comfort.

He pulled her into his embrace, warming her, too.

Yes, they had a long way to go in coming to terms with what he'd done, but she knew he was sincere in wanting her to be his wife. She knew that more than anything else now.

Soon, after arriving home, they gathered Gabriel into their circle also, sitting with him in front of the Nativity scene as they turned on a string of lights that represented the stars.

And, as Lucas held Alicia and their son to him, telling her everything she wanted to know about him, her eyes fixed on the bracelet she'd just laid to rest at the head of the bed where Baby Jesus would sleep on Christmas Eve.

A gift, she thought.

Because, in return, she'd found the best gift *she* could've ever hoped for.

Another chance at forever.

Epilogue

One year later

The family was preparing to attend late-night mass after a light meal that Alicia had cooked. The feast would come later, after the candlelight service, and Lucas's stomach was already growling at the thought of what his wife would conjure.

Last Christmas, it'd been a banquet of American and Mexican foods—everything from corn-husked tamales to enchiladas to miniburgers that Gabe had practically inhaled.

The penthouse was already redolent with the flavors of this year's offering and, as they all stood in front of the Christmas tree, guessing at what was in certain gift-wrapped presents, Lucas could tell he wasn't the only one starving.

"There's no smell like the aroma of your wife's cooking," David said, his blue eyes gleaming.

From the couch, their father chimed in. "Lucas managed to buck the Chandler trend and pick the right one the first time, didn't he?"

Gabe, dressed in church finery, giggled as his grandpa tickled him. Ever since meeting last year, the two had gotten along famously. Ford Chandler, of course, had no skill for handling difficult behavior, and Gabe seemed to sense this because he never got into one of his moods around Grandpa. True, the four-year-old had improved over the past months with the aid of his therapist and a stable home, so maybe that also had something to do with it. Still, he did have his moments, and it was always a trial for Alicia and Lucas, even if they loved Gabe to death.

When Alicia came from the direction of the kitchen, smoothing down her simple yet elegant white-velvet dress over her slightly rounded stomach, the oxygen went heavy in Lucas's lungs. He hadn't seen her wear the pristine color since their private church ceremony months ago, but he lost his ability to breathe every time he caught sight of her, anyway. A year hadn't mellowed the charged attraction between them at all.

She caught his hungry gaze, and a slow smile spread over her mouth. It was almost as if they were the only two in the room.

But leave it to David to remind him that this wasn't true.

"How'd the angel get from the top of the tree to the ground?"

As everyone laughed, Lucas caught David's gaze wandering to Alicia's growing belly. Sometimes Lucas wondered if his brother longed for love, also, but was too broken to come to terms with it. At any rate, the brothers had reached a tenuous understanding about business, David finally realizing that Lucas was at TCO to stay. The Brain had even developed a grudging respect for the way Lucas had actually turned out to be a natural at negotiating and running mergers and acquisitions—not that he would advertise that or anything.

David had also done his share of apologizing to Alicia for his part in the relationship plan, especially after he'd realized what a commodity she really was to TCO. Thanks to her, the company had introduced a prestigious charity foundation that focused on funding and building orphanages. Gradually, she'd forgiven David, just as she'd come to forgive Lucas. Lord knows he'd worked his rear end off to earn it, too. Among other things, he'd never lied to her again.

"Ready to go?" Lucas asked his wife as she stood next to him, raising her face for a kiss.

He obliged her, soft and slow, relishing every moment.

"Always ready," she said.

He rested his hand on her belly. Five months and counting. Alicia hadn't wanted to know the sex yet, so there was a lot of expectancy in the air.

"Meet you in the lobby?" David said, nudging Lucas as he left.

Lucas grunted, never taking his eyes off his wife.

"Daddy," Gabe said, running over and inserting himself between Lucas and Alicia. "Are you and Mama and baby coming?"

With a smile that he couldn't hold back, Lucas ruffled Gabe's hair as his son kissed his mom's belly.

"We're all going together."

"Yessssss," he said, doing a *Home Alone* imitation. He'd just watched the movie yesterday.

Gabe followed Uncle David and Grandpa to the foyer. But, before they left, Ford Chandler glanced back, caught his son's eye and gave him an approving smile.

Lucas had done good by falling in love. His dad had made that clear many times since last year.

He'd earned respect, all right—and it'd all come about because of Alicia. Just not the way he'd thought it would happen.

"Doing okay?" Lucas asked her as he smoothed back a curl from her brow.

She huffed out a breath, nodding. "All is well. Magdelena is seeing to the final touches of our feast."

"I'm talking about your parents." When Alicia's past would come full circle.

At the end of last year, they'd decided to hire a P.I. to track down her parents, just so she could really find closure. The crack investigator had been successful, and Alicia had made arrangements to contact each of her parents after the holidays.

"You're finally going to meet your family," he said,

drawing her against him, showing his support, his unflagging love for this woman.

"I've already met them," she said, holding him close. "I've had a true family for a while now."

As he felt her belly pressing into his hip, he reached down, resting his hand on the child they were going to cherish.

A family that had grown out of what was supposed to have been only a fake marriage.

A union that couldn't be more blessed and real.

* * * * *

Look for
MOMMY AND THE MILLIONAIRE,
the first book in Crystal Green's new miniseries,
THE SUDS CLUB
Coming in 2008
to Silhouette Special Edition.

Award-winning author, Stevi Mittman, delivers
another hysterical mystery, featuring Teddi Bayer,
an irrepressible heroine, and her to-die-for hero,
Detective Drew Scoones. After all, life on Long
Island can be murder!

*Turn the page for a sneak peek
at the warm and funny fourth book,
WHOSE NUMBER IS UP, ANYWAY?,
in the Teddi Bayer series,
by STEVI MITTMAN.
On sale August 7.*

CHAPTER 1

"Before redecorating a room, I always advise my
clients to empty it of everything but one chair.
Then I suggest they move that chair from place
to place, sitting in it, until the placement feels
right. Trust your instincts when deciding on furniture placement. Your room should "feel right."
                                    —TipsFromTeddi.com

Gut feelings. You know, that gnawing in the pit of your
stomach that warns you that you are about to do the ab-
solute stupidest thing you could do? Something that
will ruin life as you know it?

I've got one now, standing at the butcher counter in
King Kullen, the grocery store in the same strip mall
as L.I. Lanes, the bowling alley cum billiard parlor I'm
in the process of redecorating for its "Grand Opening."

I realize being in the wrong supermarket probably
doesn't sound exactly dire to you, but you aren't the one
buying your father a brisket at a store your mother will
somehow know isn't Waldbaum's.

And then, June Bayer isn't your mother.

The woman behind the counter has agreed to go into

the freezer to find a brisket for me, since there aren't any in the case. There are packages of pork tenderloin, piles of spareribs and rolls of sausage, but no briskets.

Warning Number Two, right? I should be so out of here.

But, no, I'm still in the same spot when she comes back out, brisketless, her face ashen. She opens her mouth as if she is going to scream, but only a gurgle comes out.

And then she pinballs out from behind the counter, knocking bottles of Peter Luger Steak Sauce to the floor on her way, now hitting the tower of cans at the end of the prepared foods aisle and sending them sprawling, now making her way down the aisle, careening from side to side as she goes.

Finally, from a distance, I hear her shout, "He's deeeeeeaaaad! Joey's deeeeeaaaad."

My first thought is, *You should always trust your gut.*

My second thought is that, *now, somehow, my mother will know I was in King Kullen.* For weeks, I will have to hear "What did you expect?" as though whenever you go to King Kullen someone turns up dead. And, if the detective investigating the case turns out to be Detective Drew Scoones…well, I'll never hear the end of that from her, either.

She still suspects I murdered the guy who was found dead on my doorstep last Halloween just to get Drew back into my life.

Several people head for the butcher's freezer and I position myself to block them. If there's one thing I've learned from finding people dead—and the guy on my doorstep wasn't the first one—it's that the police get very testy when you mess with their murder scenes.

"You can't go in there until the police get here," I say, stationing myself at the end of the butcher's counter and in front of the Employees Only door, acting as if I'm some sort of authority. "You'll contaminate the evidence if it turns out to be murder."

Shouts and chaos. You'd think I'd know better than to throw the word *murder* around. Cell phones are flipping open and tongues are wagging.

I amend my statement quickly. "Which, of course, it probably isn't. Murder, I mean. People die all the time, and it's not always in hospitals or their own beds, or…" I babble when I'm nervous, and the idea of someone dead on the other side of the freezer door makes me very nervous.

So does the idea of seeing Drew Scoones again. Drew and I have this on-again, off-again sort of thing… that I kind of turned off.

Who knew he'd take it so personally when he tried to get serious and I responded by saying we could talk about *us* tomorrow—and then caught a plane to my parents' condo in Boca the next day? In July. In the middle of a job.

For some crazy reason, he took that to mean that I was avoiding him and the subject of *us*.

That was three months ago. I haven't seen him since.

The manager, who identifies himself and points to his nameplate in case I don't believe him, says he has to go into *his cooler.* "Maybe Joey's not dead," he says.

"Maybe he can be saved, and you're letting him die in there. Did you ever think of that?"

In fact, I hadn't. But I had thought that the murderer might try to go back in to make sure his tracks were covered, so I say that I will go in and check.

Which means that the manager and I couple up and go in together while everyone pushes against the doorway to peer in, erasing any chance of finding clean prints on that Employees Only door.

I expect to find carcasses of dead animals hanging from hooks and maybe Joey hanging from one, too. I think it's going to be very creepy and I steel myself, only to find a rather benign series of shelves with large slabs of meat laid out carefully on them, along with boxes and boxes marked simply Chicken.

Nothing scary here, unless you count the body of a middle-aged man with graying hair sprawled faceup on the floor. His eyes are wide-open and unblinking. His shirt is stiff. His pants are stiff. His body is stiff. And his expression, you should forgive the pun—is frozen. Bill-the-manager crosses himself and stands mute while I pronounce the guy dead in a sort of *happy now?* tone.

"We should not be in here," I say, and he nods his head emphatically and helps me push people out of the doorway just in time to hear the police sirens and see the cop cars pull up outside the big store windows.

Bobbie Lyons, my partner in Teddi Bayer Interior Designs—and also my neighbor, my best friend and my private fashion police—and Mark, our carpenter—and my dogsitter, confidant and ego booster—rush in from next door. They beat the cops by a half step and shout out my name. People point in my direction.

After all the publicity that followed the unfortunate incident during which I shot my ex-husband, Rio Gallo, and then the subsequent murder of my first client—which I solved, I might add—it seems like the whole world, or, at least, all of Long Island, knows who I am.

Mark asks if I'm all right. Did I remember to mention that the man is drop-dead-gorgeous-but-a-decade-too-young-for-me-yet-too-old-for-my-daughter-thank-god? I don't get a chance to answer him because the police are quickly closing in on the store manager and me.

"The woman—" I begin telling the police. Then I have to pause for the manager to fill in her name, which he does: *Fran.*

I continue. "Right. Fran. Fran went into the freezer to get a brisket. A moment later, she came out and screamed that Joey was dead. So I'd say she was the one who discovered the body."

"And you are…" the cop asks me. It comes out a bit like who do I *think* I am, rather than who am I, really?

"An innocent bystander," Bobbie, hair perfect, makeup just right, says, carefully placing her body between the cop and me.

"And she was just leaving," Mark adds. They each take one of my arms.

Fran comes into the inner circle surrounding the cops. In case it isn't obvious from the hairnet and blood-stained white apron with *Fran* embroidered on it, I explain that she was the butcher who was going for the brisket. Mark and Bobbie take that as a signal that I've done my job and they can now get me out of there. They twist around, with me in the middle, as if we're a Rockettes line, until we are facing away from the butcher counter. They've managed to propel me a few steps toward the exit when disaster—in the form of a Mazda RX7 pulling up at the loading curb—strikes.

Mark's grip on my arm tightens like a vise. "Too late," he says.

Bobbie's expletive is unprintable. "Maybe there's a back door," she suggests, but Mark is right. It's too late.

I've laid my eyes on Detective Scoones. And, while my gut is trying to warn me that my heart shouldn't go there, regions farther south are melting at just the sight of him.

"Walk," Bobbie orders me.

And I try to. Really.

Walk, I tell my feet. *Just put one foot in front of the other.*

I can do this because I know, in my heart of hearts, that, if Drew Scoones was still interested in me, he'd have gotten in touch with me after I returned from Boca. And he hadn't.

Since he's a detective, Drew doesn't have to wear one of those dark blue Nassau County Police uniforms. Instead, he's got on jeans, a tight-fitting T-shirt and a tweedy sports jacket. If you think that sounds good, you should see him. Chiseled features, cleft chin, brown hair that's naturally a little sandy in the front, a smile that… Well, that doesn't matter. He isn't smiling now.

He walks up to me, tucks his sunglasses into his breast pocket and looks me over from head to toe.

"Well, if it isn't Miss Cut and Run," he says. "Aren't you supposed to be somewhere in Florida or something?" He looks at Mark accusingly, as if he was covering for me when he told Drew I was gone.

"Detective Scoones?" one of the uniforms says. "The stiff's in the cooler and the woman who found him is over there." He jerks his head in Fran's direction.

Drew continues to stare at me.

You know how when you were young, your mother always told you to wear clean underwear in case you were in an accident? And how, a little further on, she told you not to go out in hair rollers because you never knew who you might see—or who might see you? And how now your best friend says she wouldn't be caught dead without makeup and suggests you shouldn't, either?

Okay, today, *finally,* in my overalls and Converse sneakers, I get it.

I brush my hair out of my eyes. "Well, I'm back," I say. As if he hasn't known my exact whereabouts. The man is a detective, for heaven's sake. "Been back awhile."

Bobbie has watched the exchange and apparently decided she's given Drew all the time he deserves. "And we've got work to do, so…" she says, grabbing my arm and giving Drew a little two-fingered wave goodbye.

As I back up a foot or two, the store manager sees his chance and places himself in front of Drew, trying to get his attention. Maybe what makes Drew such a good detective is his ability to focus.

Only, what he's focusing on is me.

"Phone broken? Carrier pigeon died?" he asks me, taking in Fran, the manager, the meat counter and that Employees Only door, all without taking his eyes off me.

Mark tries to break the spell. "We've got work to do there, you've got work to do here, Scoones," Mark says to him, gesturing toward next door. "So it's back to the alley for us."

Drew's lip twitches. "You working the alley now?" he says.

"If you'd like to follow me," Bill-the-manager, clearly exasperated, says to Drew—who doesn't respond. It's as if waiting for my answer is all he has to do.

So, fine. "You knew I was back," I say.

The man has known my whereabouts every hour of the day for as long as I've known him. And my mother's not the only one who won't buy that he "just happened" to answer this particular call. In fact, I'm willing to bet my children's lunch money that he's taken every call within ten miles of my home since the day I got back.

And now he's gotten lucky.

"*You* could have called *me*," I say.

"You're the one who said *tomorrow* for our talk and then flew the coop, chickie," he says. "I figured the ball was in your court."

"Detective?" the uniform says. "There's something you ought to see in here."

Drew gives me a look that amounts to *in or out?*

He could be talking about the investigation, or about our relationship.

Bobbie tries to steer me away. Mark's fists are balled. Drew waits me out, knowing I won't be able to resist what might be a murder investigation.

Finally, he turns and heads for the cooler.

And, like a puppy dog, I follow.

Bobbie grabs the back of my shirt and pulls me to a halt.

"I'm just going to show him something," I say, yanking away.

"Yeah," Bobbie says, pointedly looking at the buttons on my blouse. The two at breast level have popped. "That's what I'm afraid of."

REQUEST YOUR FREE BOOKS!
2 FREE NOVELS PLUS 2 FREE GIFTS!

SPECIAL EDITION®
Life, Love and Family!

YES! Please send me 2 FREE Silhouette Special Edition® novels and my 2 FREE gifts. After receiving them, if I don't wish to receive any more books, I can return the shipping statement marked "cancel." If I don't cancel, I will receive 6 brand-new novels every month and be billed just $4.24 per book in the U.S., or $4.99 per book in Canada, plus 25¢ shipping and handling per book and applicable taxes, if any*. That's a savings of at least 15% off the cover price! I understand that accepting the 2 free books and gifts places me under no obligation to buy anything. I can always return a shipment and cancel at any time. Even if I never buy another book from Silhouette, the two free books and gifts are mine to keep forever.

235 SDN EEYU   335 SDN EEY6

Name _____ (PLEASE PRINT)

Address _____ Apt. _____

City _____ State/Prov. _____ Zip/Postal Code _____

Signature (if under 18, a parent or guardian must sign)

Mail to the **Silhouette Reader Service™:**
IN U.S.A.: P.O. Box 1867, Buffalo, NY 14240-1867
IN CANADA: P.O. Box 609, Fort Erie, Ontario L2A 5X3

Not valid to current Silhouette Special Edition subscribers.

Want to try two free books from another line?
Call 1-800-873-8635 or visit www.morefreebooks.com.

* Terms and prices subject to change without notice. NY residents add applicable sales tax. Canadian residents will be charged applicable provincial taxes and GST. This offer is limited to one order per household. All orders subject to approval. Credit or debit balances in a customer's account(s) may be offset by any other outstanding balance owed by or to the customer. Please allow 4 to 6 weeks for delivery.

Your Privacy: Silhouette is committed to protecting your privacy. Our Privacy Policy is available online at www.eHarlequin.com or upon request from the Reader Service. From time to time we make our lists of customers available to reputable firms who may have a product or service of interest to you. If you would prefer we not share your name and address, please check here. ☐

SSE07

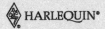

COMING NEXT MONTH